'But I don't wan
finally burst out
interested in it. O

'Methinks you doth protest too much,' he taunted. 'Hebe, the bottom line is I now have a responsibility to you and the baby.'

A responsibility? Was that what she had become? After years of independence, of paying her own way, was that what she was going to be reduced to? No, she wouldn't become that! No matter how difficult going it alone was going to be, she wouldn't become that...

She gave a firm shake of her head. 'I don't need or want your help, thank you,' she told him stiffly.

'Haven't you understood yet, Hebe?' Nick ground out fiercely. 'I'm not asking, I'm *telling* you how it's going to be!'

Hebe raised her head to look at him numbly. 'What do you mean?'

'Simply that I am going to marry you, Hebe,' he told her grimly. 'Just as quickly as the arrangements can be made!'

Carole Mortimer was born in England, the youngest of three children. She began writing in 1978, and has now written over ninety books for Harlequin Mills and Boon®. Carole has four sons, Matthew, Joshua, Timothy and Peter, and a bearded collie called Merlyn. She says, 'I'm happily married to Peter senior; we're best friends as well as lovers, which is probably the best recipe for a successful relationship.'

Recent titles by the same author:

THE CHRISTMAS NIGHT MIRACLE
THE INNOCENT VIRGIN

PREGNANT BY
THE MILLIONAIRE

BY
CAROLE MORTIMER

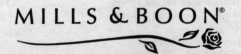

All the characters in this book have no existence outside the imagination of the author, and have no relation whatsoever to anyone bearing the same name or names. They are not even distantly inspired by any individual known or unknown to the author, and all the incidents are pure invention.

First published in Great Britain 2006
Paperback edition 2007
Harlequin Mills & Boon Limited,
Eton House, 18-24 Paradise Road, Richmond, Surrey TW9 1SR

© Carole Mortimer 2006

ISBN-13: 978 0 263 85299 8
ISBN-10:   0 263 85299 7

Set in Times Roman 10½ on 12¾ pt
01-0207-48159

Printed and bound in Spain
by Litografia Rosés, S.A., Barcelona

PREGNANT
BY THE
MILLIONAIRE

CHAPTER ONE

NICK woke up alone.

Which was strange, because he was pretty sure he hadn't been alone when he'd fallen into a satiated asleep several hours ago.

Something about a goddess…?

Ah, yes—Hebe, the goddess of youth.

Tall, slender, with a long, straight curtain of silver-blonde hair and eyes of so pale a brown they were gold. Strange magnetic eyes, that gleamed with a multitude of secrets.

Not that he was interested in learning those secrets. Hebe had merely been a distraction, a way of putting the past and all the pain and the significance of the day behind him. He had wanted to forget, be diverted, and the presence of Hebe Johnson had certainly provided that. For a few hours, at least.

So where was she? It was still dark outside, and the tangled sheets beside him were still warm, so she couldn't have been gone long.

He frowned slightly at the thought of her having just disappeared into the night. That was usually *his* privilege! Wine, dine and bed a woman, but never ever become involved—least of all allow them into the inner privacy of his life.

Of course that was slightly more difficult when it was his bed they had shared!

Because she didn't live alone, he remembered now. Something about a flatmate. So after dinner he had brought her back to his apartment over the gallery for a drink instead— and other things!—breaking his cardinal rule in the bargain.

Two rules, in fact, he acknowledged with a grimace as he remembered that Hebe actually worked for him, two floors down, in the Cavendish Gallery on the ground floor.

But desperate times called for desperate measures, and so he had brought Hebe back here, needing to lose himself in the lithe beauty of her perfect, long-limbed body. And he had. He'd found himself dazzled, bewitched—the fact that she wasn't one of the sophisticated women who usually had a brief place in his life, adding to the excitement of the evening. To the point that his pain had been anaesthetised, if not completely erased.

Nick gave a groan as he remembered what yesterday signified, moving to sit up in the bed, needing to get away from the scene of that heated lovemaking now, and standing up to turn his back on those tumbled sheets before walking out of the bedroom.

Only to come to an abrupt halt as he saw he wasn't alone after all.

Hebe, the goddess, was just switching the light off as she came out of the kitchen with a glass of water in her hand, her nakedness only shielded by the fine silver-blonde hair that reached almost to her waist.

Nick instantly felt a stirring of renewed arousal as he looked at that golden body—legs long and silky, hips and waist slenderly curvaceous, breasts firm and uptilting, the nipples rosily pouting.

As if begging to be kissed. Again.

He had noticed her at the gallery several months ago, her beauty such that it was impossible for her not to stand out. But he hadn't so much as spoken to her until yesterday.

And now he wanted her. Again.

'What are you doing?' he prompted huskily as he padded softly across the room to join her, with only a small table-light for illumination.

Hebe's breath caught in her throat just at the sight of him. She was still not quite sure how she had ended up in Nick Cavendish's apartment. In his bed. In his arms.

She had been captivated by him since the moment she'd first seen him. In love, or more probably in lust, she acknowledged ruefully as she easily remembered each kiss and caress of the previous night, having been totally lost from the first moment Nick had held her in his arms and touched her.

Or perhaps she had been lost before that…

An American, the charismatic Nick Cavendish owned the London art gallery where she worked, as well as others in Paris and New York. His time was equally divided between the three, with apartments on the top floor of each building always ready for his use.

Hebe had been working at the gallery for several weeks before she'd first caught a glimpse of the elusive owner.

When he'd walked forcefully into the west room of the gallery four months ago, seemingly filled with boundless energy as he fired instructions one of the managers, Hebe had felt as if all the air had been knocked out of her lungs.

Over six feet tall, his body lithe and muscular, with overlong dark hair swept back from his olive-skinned face, and eyes a deep, deep blue, there was a wild ruggedness about him that spoke of the energy of a caged tiger. With the same threat of danger!

But she had never in her wildest dreams imagined he would notice her, a lowly junior employee. She had been leaving the gallery the evening before when she'd accidentally walked straight into him, but instead of getting a scornful look, as she had expected, they had both laughed and apologized. Still, she'd been totally stunned when he'd asked if she would join him for dinner, on the basis that she had worked at the gallery for some months now and it was time the two of them became acquainted.

Became acquainted!

They had become a lot more than that last night. Hebe was sure that not an inch of her body hadn't known the intimate touch of his hands or lips.

Her cheeks were flushed now with the memory of that intimacy.

And at the naked perfection of his body now. A body, as she had discovered the previous evening, that had that olive tan all over, a light covering of dark hair on the muscular width of his chest, and down over powerful hips and thighs.

As she saw the renewed state of his arousal, she felt a liquid melting between her own thighs as heat coursed through her already languorous body.

'I hope you don't mind—I was thirsty,' she answered him huskily, holding up the glass of water she had been drinking from.

Nick was thirsty too—but not for water. Taking the glass out of her hand, he placed it on a table, his eyes darkening as his head lowered to kiss one enticing nipple. He looked up into Hebe's face as he stroked his tongue moistly over that sensitive tip, feeling the increasing hardness of his own body as she groaned low in her throat, eyes gleaming like molten gold as her body arched against him, dark lashes sweeping low over her flushed cheeks.

She was beautiful, this goddess of youth, and he wanted to lose himself in her once again. Not to blot out the painful memories of yesterday this time, but because he wanted her with a fierceness that told him he wouldn't be gentle with her. That he couldn't be. He needed to drive his body into hers, but knew she would meet that desire with a heat of her own. As she had before.

He straightened to swing her up into his arms, capturing her mouth with his, tongue plundering, as her arms moved up about his neck, her fingers becoming entangled in the darkness of his hair.

Hebe was trembling as he laid her down amidst the twisted sheets, his mouth deepening its possession of hers as one of his hands caressed the burning tip of her breast, the nipple already hard and aroused, sending sensations of heat and liquid fire through the rest of her body.

She restlessly caressed the broad width of his back, before trailing a path to the firmness of his thighs, touching him there, loving the feel of his hardness against her hand. The groan low in his throat assured her that he approved too.

Nick fell back against the pillows as Hebe began to kiss his chest, down to the hollow of his flat stomach, and even lower over the hardness of his thighs. His breath caught in his throat as he felt the sensuous flick of her tongue against his heated flesh, and at the same time he knew that he wouldn't be able to take too much of this, that he wanted to be between the engulfing warmth of her thighs, inside her, stroking them both to that shuddering climax that he remembered so clearly—twice—from the night before.

He moved above her, looking down into her aroused face as he slowly entered her, her hips moving up to meet his, taking him deep inside her as she began to move slowly against him.

Hebe gasped minutes—hours?—later, as she felt the pleasure pulsing hotly through her, her body shuddering and quivering as that pleasure erupted out of control, taking her with it.

Taking Nick with it too, pulsating deep and deliciously inside her as he surrendered to the sensations of his body.

Hebe lay with her head resting against his chest in the aftermath, his arm about her waist, holding her loosely at his side.

She had never experienced anything like this. Their bodies seemed completely in tune, their lovemaking almost balletic in its intensity of emotion.

She smiled to herself as she realised how happy she felt, how totally relaxed and fulfilled. She really could so easily fall completely, mindlessly, in love with this man. If she wasn't already!

Which, considering her uninhibited response to him, she had a feeling she just might be.

Whatever, she felt closer to him than she ever had to anyone before, and wondered what the future held for them. Would they spend the day together? It was Sunday, so neither of them had to be at work today. Maybe they would make breakfast together? Before making love. Then perhaps they would go for a walk in the nearby park. Before making love. And then they could…

Hebe, exhausted and happy, drifted off to sleep.

Nick lay sleepless beside her, his body filled with satiation but his mind suddenly crystal clear.

Hebe Johnson was beautiful and desirable, and responded to him in a completely uninhibited way that he found irresistable. But it was her lack of control that warned him he *had* to resist her. Not for him the silken shackles of any woman, the cosy togetherness that tightened those ties until no thought or action could be called his own. Never again. That way lay all the pain and despair he had tried so hard to blot out the night before.

And she was still his employee. Untouchable, in fact. Though he had already done a hell of a lot more than touch her!

Creating a situation he had always avoided in the past.

Since his divorce two years ago he had known lots of women, had wined and dined them, bedded them, and moved on without any regrets. None of those relationships had lasted long enough to forge any sort of bond, least of all an emotional one. But an employee, as he had always known and therefore avoided, was going to be a little more difficult to walk away from.

But he was going to do it anyway. Walk away and not look back.

Quite what he'd do about the fact that Hebe worked for him he wasn't sure yet. The easiest way would be to dispense with her services at the gallery. But it didn't seem quite fair that she should lose her job because she had gone to bed with him. In fact, most women would assume their job was *more* secure after going to bed with the boss!

He turned slightly to look at her as she slept in his arms. Was that the reason Hebe had come so willingly with him the night before? The reason she had come back here and made love with him?

If it was, she was in for a nasty surprise!

No one, and nothing, held Nick Cavendish any more—least of all a silver-haired siren with golden eyes.

Hebe felt almost shy as she came into the ultra-modern kitchen several hours later.

Having woken up alone in Nick Cavendish's huge four-poster bed, with the disarray of the bedclothes a stark reminder of the heated lovemaking that had taken place there both last night and earlier this morning—as if she needed any reminder—she had collected up her scattered clothes and gone through to the luxury of the adjoining bathroom to shower and dress before going in search of Nick.

He was here, in the spacious kitchen, his back towards her as he made coffee, having pulled on faded denims and a black tee shirt over his nakedness.

Hebe looked at him, watching the muscles rippling in the broadness of his back as he moved, his shoulder-length dark hair brushed back to curl loosely against the nape of his neck.

Aged thirty-eight—twelve years older than her own twenty-six—he was without doubt the most gorgeous man she had ever seen. All over, she remembered with a plea-surable flush. Not an ounce of superfluous flesh on his body, and his hands—those hands that had caressed her so thoroughly—were long and tapered. And he made love with an artistry that spoke of an experience she came nowhere near matching.

Of course he had been married. For five years, according to Kate, another assistant at the gallery. Hebe had learnt this after Nick's second whirlwind visit three months ago, when he had snapped and snarled at them all before disappearing again on his way to terrorise the staff at his Paris gallery.

Kate had explained that he could be like that sometimes—that there had been a son from the marriage, a little boy who had died when he was only four. His death had precipitated the break-up and divorce of his parents two years ago, and still sometimes sent Nick Cavendish spiralling into a inferno of dark emotions that seemed to find no outlet.

Not surprising, really. Hebe could imagine nothing more traumatic than the death of your young child. But these intriguing snatches of information about her employer had only increased her interest in this enigmatically charismatic man.

She had watched him covertly during his lightning visits to the gallery. She had seen him dark and brooding as on that second visit, and smiling occasionally, but once laughing outright, which had softened and smoothed the lines of experience from his face, making him look almost boyish. Except for the deep well of pain never far from those intense blue eyes.

So he swept sporadically into the gallery, bringing his life and vitality with him, inspiring the people around him with his intensity, fascinating and intriguing Hebe—before once again disappearing and taking all that vitality with him.

But never in Hebe's wildest dreams had she ever imagined he would invite her out to dinner in the way that he had, that she would spend the night here with him in his apartment.

Nick sensed rather than heard Hebe's entrance into the kitchen, and he was aware of her silence as she stood in the doorway behind him whilst he continued to prepare the coffee, to delay the moment when they would have to make conversation. Conversation, he found, served very little purpose after spending the night with a woman.

To him, the following morning had always been the worst part of the brief, unfocused relationships he had indulged in before and since his divorce. What were you supposed to talk about, for God's sake? The weather? Who was going to win the tennis championship this year? The big U.S. golf tournament? Hardly post-lovemaking conversation topics, any of them!

But the alternative was discussing when they would see each other again—and that was just as unacceptable to Nick. Especially in this case. He knew now that he had made a terrible mistake in getting involved with Hebe Johnson, and certainly didn't intend compounding the situation by pretending this relationship—one-night-stand?—had any future.

Oh, well—time to face the music, Nick decided impatiently, and he turned to face her. The quicker he got this over with, the sooner he would be able to get on with his life.

She was once again dressed in the black silk blouse and fitted black trousers she had worn the day before, her hair falling silkily about her shoulders, her make-up attempting, and not quite succeeding, to hide the slight redness to her chin, where his late-night stubble and the intensity of their kisses had scratched that delicate creamy skin.

He wasn't even going to go there! No more thoughts of how wild and willing this woman had been in his arms. Otherwise he would just end up taking her back to bed again.

'Ready to leave?' he questioned dismissively as he took in her appearance. 'Or would you like a cup of coffee before you go?' He held up the coffeepot.

Hebe frowned at his abruptness. He couldn't wait to get rid of her, could he? So much for her imaginings of them spending the day together, talking together, laughing together, making love again…!

'I—don't think so, thank you,' she refused uncertainly, wondering if he really just expected her to leave now that the night was over.

An awkward silence followed.

What was she waiting for? Nick wondered impatiently. He had offered her coffee, she had refused, now it would be better for both of them if she just—

'I—perhaps I had better be going.' She spoke awkwardly as she seemed to sense his unspoken urging. Questioningly. As if she expected him to ask her to stay.

For what reason? They'd had dinner. They'd made love. They'd both enjoyed it. And now it was over. What else did she want from him? Because he had nothing else to give!

'My flatmate will probably be wondering where I've got to,' she added with a frown.

Nick hadn't bothered to ask last night whether that flatmate was male or female. He had been too caught up in smothering, numbing, his own inner pain, to care.

But he felt curious now, and wondered if Hebe Johnson were engaged, or at least had a steady boyfriend. She didn't come over as the sort of woman who indulged in extra-relationship affairs. But then, she hadn't exactly come over as the sort of woman who would go to bed with him last night either—and look how wrong he had been about that!

This was extremely awkward, Hebe decided uncomfortably as she continued to stand in the doorway, having no idea how she was supposed to behave the-morning-after-the-night-before. Probably because it was a long time since there had *been* a morning-after-the-night-before for her!

Not that she was a complete innocent—she had been in a relationship years ago, when she was at university. But she had never stayed in a man's apartment all night before, and as this man was Nick Cavendish, her employer for the last six months, it was doubly awkward.

He merely looked relieved at her suggestion that she leave. 'If you're sure you don't want coffee?' he prompted dismissively, as he poured some coffee into a mug for himself—black, with no sugar.

The repeat of the offer was made more out of politeness than anything else, Hebe realised with a sinking of her heart, as Nick sat down at the breakfast bar to take a sip of the steaming brew, no longer even looking at her.

She had been completely overwhelmed by the attention of this ruggedly handsome, gorgeously seductive man the night before, and hadn't been able to believe her luck when he had seemed to return her interest. But it looked as if she might have plenty of time to repent at leisure if his distant behaviour now was anything to go by.

Her cue not to make this any more embarrassing than it already was…

'I'll go, then,' she announced brightly. 'I—thank you for dinner last night,' she added awkwardly.

And everything else, she could have added, but didn't. After the intimacies they had shared the night before, this really was too embarrassingly awful. Something she didn't intend ever to repeat if this was what it felt like the following morning.

She looked a little bewildered by his abruptness, Nick acknowledged with a certain guilty irritation after glancing at her. Those amazing gold-coloured eyes were wide with wariness, and her cheeks had gone slightly pale at his obvious lack of enthusiasm.

What had she expected, for goodness' sake? That he would make declarations of undying love for her this morning? Assure her he couldn't live without her and invite her to come along with him to New York when he left later this morning?

Damn it, this was real life—not some fairy story. And they were adults, not romantic children!

They had both had a good time, but that was all it had been.

'I'm going back to New York later on today,' he told her dismissively. 'But I'll give you a call, okay?' he added—knowing he had no intention of doing any such thing.

He should never have become personally involved with an employee in the first place, so he certainly didn't intend to arrange to see Hebe Johnson on a social level again.

For one thing, he knew that if he met up with Hebe again, away from the gallery, then they would end up in bed together again too. Even now, looking at the soft pout of her mouth, that quicksilver hair, the willowy curves of her body in the silky blouse and fitted black trousers, he felt the stirring of desire for her—an ache he was absolutely determined to do nothing about.

She was definitely being given the brush-off, Hebe realised painfully. She wasn't so naïve that she didn't know that when a man said *I'll call you* after spending the night, without so much as asking for your telephone number, it meant that he had no intention of ever contacting you again!

Of course Nick was slightly different, in that he could, if he wanted, get her telephone number from Personnel at the Cavendish Gallery. She just didn't think, from his dismissive attitude this morning, that he was ever going to want to.

The excitement of having dinner with him last night, and the hours they had spent making love, and now being summararily dismissed this morning had ultimately to be the most humiliating experience of her entire life.

She couldn't get out of here fast enough!

She looked as if she were going to make a mad dash out of here without so much as a goodbye, Nick realised. Well, that was what he wanted, wasn't it? He frowned unwittingly, acknowledging that he didn't enjoy being on the receiving end of a casual dismissal. *He* was always the one to bid farewell, not the other way round.

He stood up, smiling slightly as he crossed the kitchen to put his arms about Hebe's waist and pull her into the hardness of his body. 'Goodbye, Hebe!' he murmured, his arousal undeniable.

She looked up at him, five or six inches shorter than his own six feet two inches in height, her eyes golden globes of uncertainty.

Hell, she had beautiful eyes, Nick thought with an inward groan. Beautiful everything, if his memory didn't deceive him. And he knew that it didn't.

Maybe they could meet again after all—

No! Don't be an idiot, Nick, he rebuked himself impatiently. Much better to just leave it like this.

Leave it, and hope that with time they would both forget last night had ever happened…

He certainly intended doing exactly that!

CHAPTER TWO

Six weeks later Hebe was still waiting for the promised telephone call from Nick Cavendish.

She had been a fool ever to expect that he would phone, of course, and several conversations with Kate over the last few weeks had confirmed that Nick Cavendish did not get seriously involved with any of the women he went out with. The number of women he had been involved with since the end of his marriage, also according to Kate, had been legion, and none of them, Kate had told her wistfully—as if she'd guessed Hebe's interest was more than casual—had ever been employees of the Cavendish Galleries.

Or if they had they very quickly hadn't been, Hebe had decided.

In fact, she had lived most of the last six weeks half expecting to be told her employment at the Cavendish Gallery had been terminated. Of course it wasn't as easy as that to get rid of people nowadays, but she didn't doubt that if he wanted her out of here, Nick Cavendish would find a way.

The fact that he was—at last!—due back at the London gallery next week, in time for the opening of an exhibition they were giving was not conducive to helping Hebe concentrate on her work.

In fact, she felt decidedly clumsy today, and had been dropping things most of the morning, not seeming to be co-ordinated at all. Of course she knew the reason for her steadily increasing nervousness. Nick's arrival next week was approaching with a speed that made her head spin.

Maybe she should have called in sick for a few days. She was certainly feeling more than a little green round the edges, and hadn't even been able to eat at all today. Her anxiety at the prospect of seeing Nick again seemed to be increasing daily.

Although why *she* should be the one to feel so nervously on edge was beyond her. After all, Nick Cavendish had been the one to invite her out, not the other way round. And she hadn't invited herself back to his apartment either. In fact—

'Hebe?' rasped an all too familiar voice after six weeks' silence close to her ear.

She spun round sharply, at the same time dropping the name cards she had been preparing for next week's exhi-bition.

'Sorry!' she muttered, and she bent to pick them up with shaking fingers, taking the few seconds to bring some composure back to her demeanour.

Nick wasn't expected until *next week!*

'What are you doing here?' she prompted slowly as she straightened, eyes deeply golden in the paleness of her face.

He returned her gaze mockingly. 'It may have escaped your memory, Hebe, but I happen to own this gallery and have an apartment on the top floor of the building; I can come here any time I damn well please!'

Well…yes… But if she had had prior notice of his earlier than expected arrival she might not have overreacted in the way she just had. As it was, she felt completely wrong-footed.

She had made her mind up, during Nick's six weeks of silence, that she was going to be cool and composed when he did come back and would make no reference, if he didn't, to the fact that they had spent the night together in his apartment on the top floor of the building…

'Let's go up to my office,' Nick added with barely concealed impatience. 'I want to talk to you.'

He looked just the same, she acknowledged achingly. His olive skin was just as healthily tanned, his blue eyes as sharply intelligent, and his dark hair, though looking as if it had been trimmed slightly, was still long enough to rest silkily on broad shoulders. Dressed formally in a dark grey suit and snowy white shirt, with a silver-grey silk tie knotted neatly at his throat, he looked like a man who was firmly in control.

He looked exactly what he was, in fact—the confident multimillionaire owner of three prestigious art galleries.

Looking at him now, Hebe wondered how she could ever have thought he was seriously interested in her!

'Hebe!' he prompted, frowning at her continued silence.

She was behaving like an idiot, she realised, just standing here staring at him, completely tongue-tied by his unexpected appearance in the gallery.

She drew in a deep breath, willing herself to behave naturally. Well, as naturally as it was possible to be when confronted by the man who had haunted her days and filled her dreams for last six weeks!

'What can I do for you, Mr Cavendish?' she prompted with calm efficiency.

'You can come upstairs to my office with me,' he repeated firmly. 'Now!' he added, not even waiting for her answer this time, but turning abruptly on his heel and striding forcefully out of the room.

Kate, who was working nearby, shot Hebe a questioning look as she trailed out of the gallery behind Nick, and Hebe gave her a how-should-I-know? shrug in reply.

Because she really *didn't* know what this was about. They had had dinner together, spent a night together, but she hadn't told anyone about either of those things, let alone tried to contact Nick himself. So what was his problem?

The more she thought about it, acknowledging his brooding silence as he lithely climbed the stairs ahead of her to his office on the second floor, the angrier she became.

Had he expected, on the basis that she had spent the night with the boss, that she would have left her job here before he returned? Was that the reason he was so angry? Because he hadn't expected to see her still here at all?

Well, that was being more than a little unfair, wasn't it?

She loved her job here, liked the people she worked with too. Besides, none of the awkwardness of this situation was *her* fault, damn it!

Nick eyed her irritably as he closed his office door behind them. Unless he was mistaken, from her flushed cheeks and glowing golden eyes, he would take a guess at her being one very indignant young lady.

He perched on the edge of his cool Italian marble desk, which more than one customer at the gallery had tried to buy from him. He had always refused to sell it, though, liking the way it complemented the rest of the room, which was wood-panelled and slightly austere, although it did have a huge picture window that looked out over the river.

'So, what are you so angry about, Hebe?' he drawled ruefully, dark brows raised over mocking blue eyes. 'The fact that I was less than polite just now? Or the fact that I haven't called you for two months?' He met her gaze challengingly.

'Six weeks,' she came back sharply, her cheeks flushing with colour seconds later.

'Whatever.' He shrugged, knowing exactly how long it was since he had last seen her, but having no intention of letting Hebe know that he did.

He had been so sure that Hebe Johnson would be just like all the other women he had known over the last two years—taken and then forgotten. But for some inexplicable reason he hadn't quite succeeded in doing that where she was concerned. Memories of those golden eyes, that lithe silken body, came flashing into his mind at the most inconvenient of times. Irritating him intensely.

The flash of anger now in the depths of her warm eyes, and the way the fullness of those sensuous lips had tightened slightly, told him his careless attitude had only succeeded in increasing her anger. Which didn't particularly affect him.

Not on a business level, anyway.

On a personal level, he found both things sexy as hell!

She looked good today too, dressed in a cream blouse tucked into the tiny waistband of a knee-length fitted black skirt, her legs long and silky.

So much for his absence from the London gallery these last six weeks, his deliberate lack of the promised telephone call, his self-assurances that when he came back he would have forgotten all about Hebe Johnson!

Even before he'd seen the painting he had known he hadn't managed to do that.

His own mouth tightened as he glanced over to where he had placed the painting, on a stand to one side of his wide office, with a cover over it to protect it. But also so that Hebe Johnson shouldn't see it until he was ready for her to do so…

Hebe eyed Nick scathingly as he stood looking at her, and, even though inside was shaking, she gripped her hands tightly together to prevent Nick from seeing they were trembling.

'I'm sorry—were you supposed to call me?' she came back, with all the coolness she could muster.

Which was quite considerable, if the way his mouth thinned and his eyes narrowed to glittering blue slits was anything to go by!

'Okay, Hebe, forget that for the moment,' he dismissed briskly. 'And tell me what you know about Andrew Southern?'

She frowned as she dredged her memory for the relevant facts about the artist, having no idea why Nick was asking the question—unless it was an effort on his part to prove that she didn't know her job, so giving him an excuse to fire her?

She swallowed hard. 'English. Born 1953. Started painting in his early twenties, mainly portraits, but later moved on to landscapes—more recently the Alaskan wilderness—'

'I'm not asking for a bio on the guy, Hebe!' Nick cut in tersely, standing up restlessly. 'I asked what *you* know about him?'

'Me?' She blinked, stepping back slightly in the face of his leashed vitality. 'I've just told you what I know about him—'

'Don't be so coy, Hebe,' he cut her off again abruptly, blue eyes mocking. 'I'm not asking for details, just a confirmation that you know him. And if you can contact him personally.'

She was totally bewildered now. This conversation didn't appear to have anything to do with that night six weeks ago at all, nor with an effort to prove her incompetent, but everything, it seemed, to do with the artist Andrew Southern. Of whom she was an admirer, but had certainly never met him, let alone knew him personally.

She wasn't going to acknowledge the relationship, Nick realized frustratedly. Well, the guy was old enough to be her father, so maybe that explained her reluctance to talk about him. Whatever, Nick had been trying to arrange a meeting with Andrew Southern for years. For once neither the name Nick Cavendish nor the Cavendish Galleries themselves had opened that particular door. And now it seemed that Hebe, of all people, might be the key to that meeting.

From deciding that he had to stay as far away from Hebe as possible in future, or else take her to his bed again, he had now discovered that if he wanted to get anywhere near Andrew Southern with the idea of an exhibition of his work, then Hebe was the person he had to talk to.

'Look, Hebe, let's start this conversation again, shall we?' he reasoned pleasantly. 'I accept that I overstepped the employer/employee line with you six weeks ago, but by the same token you have to accept that it wasn't all one sided, huh?'

Hebe eyed him derisively. If that was his attempt at an apology for the night they had spent together, or for his non-existent telephone call since, then it was pretty lame. Besides which, an apology for the former was insulting, to say the least, just as an off-hand apology for the latter was totally inadequate.

She had been so miserable these last six weeks, wondering where she had gone wrong, what she had done to make Nick Cavendish not even want to call her again, let alone see her.

And now he had turned up unexpectedly, dismissing their night together as the satisfying of a brief, mutual attraction, before going on to talk about Andrew Southern—an artist of phenomenal reputation, and known as a complete recluse, who had been so for almost thirty years.

Making her realise just how little she understood Nick Cavendish.

She eyed him coolly now. 'Is that all?'

'No, of course—!' He broke off to draw in a deeply controlling breath. 'Are you deliberately trying to annoy me?' He looked at her with narrowed eyes.

She gave a mocking lift of her eyebrows. 'I seem to be doing that without trying!'

He relaxed slightly, an amused smile slightly curving those sculptured lips. 'I see now why I found you so intriguing that night,' he murmured softly.

It wasn't what she wanted to hear. Not here. Not now.

She had spent the first week after his departure back to New York in a frenzy of self-recrimination, with a deep-felt need for Nick to call her to nullify all those negative thoughts.

She was in love with him, totally physically enthralled with him—and this was the twenty-first century, for goodness' sake, not the Dark Ages, where a woman's wants and needs weren't considered as important as a man's, she had chided herself.

She had done nothing wrong by spending the night with a man she found so attractive and who had wanted her too!

But as the days and weeks had passed those assurances hadn't meant a whole lot.

And now standing here looking at Nick, they meant absolutely nothing.

She grimaced. 'I think it might be better if we both just forgot about that, don't you?'

It was a statement rather than a question, and Nick found himself deeply irritated by her easy dismissal.

Okay, so he hadn't been able to wait to get her out of his apartment that morning six weeks ago, and he hadn't called her as he said he would, but it was a bit of knock to his ego to realise that she was willing to dismiss the memories of him as easily as he had tried to dismiss her.

Or was she…?

He took a step towards her, lids lowered as he looked down at her with dark blue eyes, trailing one caressing finger down the smooth curve of her cheek. 'Am I so easy to forget, Hebe?' he murmured seductively, knowing that this was probably another mistake, but finding her coolness infuriating as hell. 'Was our love-making easy to forget too? Or has it kept you awake nights, thinking of all the ways we touched and aroused each other?'

She gave him a startled look even as the colour entered her cheeks, her lips parting slightly as her body swayed towards his.

'I thought so…' He murmured his satisfaction with her response, his wandering fingers parting her lips slightly, caressing that softness, before trailing the length of her throat down to the deep vee of her blouse and the creamy swell of her breasts. All the time his challenging gaze continued to hold hers.

How could this be happening? Hebe inwardly protested, even as she felt herself responding to his touch. The arousal of her breasts was instant, the nipples hard and sensitive, as she reached out instinctively to cling tightly to the broad width of his shoulders, her legs seeming in danger of melting beneath her.

But as suddenly as he had touched her she found herself thrust away from him, and Nick was stepping back, that devilishly handsome face now set in scathing dismissal.

'You really are a sexy little thing, aren't you?' he mused as he leant back against his desk, his blue gaze considering now, as he looked at the firm thrust of her breasts against her cream blouse.

'Mr Cavendish—'

'Oh, come on, Hebe,' he drawled tauntingly, shaking his head slightly, those blue eyes alight with mocking laughter. 'You can hardly go back to calling me *that* after sharing your body with me,' he reminded her, with a challenging rise of that square, uncompromising chin.

Hebe felt the colour warm her cheeks at his deliberate taunting. Why was he doing this to her? What perverse pleasure did he get out of humiliating her in this way?

She straightened defensively, glaring at him. 'At the same time as *you* shared your body with *me*!' she came back, with all the fury of her humiliation, uncaring now if this was just his way of trying to get her to resign from her job at the gallery.

Fine. Let him sack her. She was quickly reaching the point where she didn't care.

His smile was derisive. 'I'm flattered that amongst all your other lovers you've even remembered me.'

All her other—! What was he talking about? She had had one relationship before him, and that had been five years ago; ancient history rather than recent.

'Let's stop playing this game, shall we?' Nick said impatiently as he stood up.

'Gladly!' she agreed tautly. 'Can I go back to work now?' If she didn't get out of here soon she was very much afraid the humiliating tears that blurred her vision would escape and begin to fall hotly down her cheeks!

'No, you damn well—' Nick broke off abruptly, drawing in controlling breaths as he realised she had to be deliberately baiting him.

Because he knew of her relationship with Andrew Southern?

Probably, he accepted scathingly. Okay, so as an artist the man was a legend in his own lifetime, but he was still a man aged in his fifties, and Hebe was only in her midtwenties. And Nick had wondered if *he* was too old for her!

'Okay, Hebe,' he began reasoningly. 'I accept that your affair with Andrew Southern is none of my business—'

'My *what*?' she gasped incredulously, gold eyes wide with disbelief.

'It's past history, I realise that—'

'Past—!' Hebe gave a dazed shake of her head. 'But I told you. I don't even *know* Andrew Southern!' she protested indignantly.

'Evidence proves the contrary—'

'Evidence?' she repeated disgustedly. 'Look, Nick, I have no idea what you're talking about.' She shook her head, that amazing silver-blonde hair moving silkily against her creamy cheeks. 'Maybe you have jet-lag, and it's affecting your judgement. I don't know, but—'

'I came back from New York last week, Hebe,' he told her softly, his gaze narrowing as she looked at him sharply. 'I'd received information that there was a possibility of a hitherto unseen Andrew Southern coming up for sale in the north of England.' His mouth twisted. 'As you can imagine, I had no intention of letting anyone but Cavendish Galleries own that painting.'

'For Cavendish Galleries read Nick Cavendish!' she came back scathingly.

'Exactly.' He smiled in acknowledgement of her derision. 'Imagine my surprise when I saw the subject of the painting!'

Hebe gave a dazed shake of her head. She had no idea what this conversation was about, or where it could possibly be going. But Nick, it seemed, had been back in England a week already. A week during which he had neither telephoned her nor tried to see her again.

Until today. When he had done nothing but humiliate and embarrass her.

But he had taken her in his arms too...

To prove a point. Nothing else. And he *had* proved it too, hadn't he? She responded to him even when she didn't want to.

Sometimes she wasn't sure if she didn't hate him rather than love him!

'The subject of the painting...?' she prompted frowningly.

'Yes.' Nick was looking at her with narrowed eyes now. 'A portrait. A woman. A very beautiful woman, in fact.' He shrugged his broad shoulders as if that point was indisputable.

'It's one of his earlier paintings then—?'

'No,' Nick cut in with certainty. 'I can categorically say this work is recent. The last five years or so, I would say,' he added consideringly.

'But I thought he didn't paint portraits any more—'

'Obviously this woman inspired him to do so,' Nick cut in dryly.

Hebe didn't like the way he was looking at her now, as if critically dissecting every part of her body.

A body he had come to know intimately six weeks ago...

Except he hadn't seemed to find anything to critisise about it then, had he?

She shrugged. 'As far as I'm aware, Andrew Southern hasn't painted a portrait for over twenty years.'

'Are you doubting my expertise, Hebe?' Nick snapped tautly.

No, she wasn't doing that. Not in any way! She knew only too well what an masterful lover he was. And he hadn't built up the prestigious worldwide reputation of the Cavendish Galleries by not being extremely knowledgable about art. He knew his subject equally as well as he knew how to be a lover!

Nick was growing tired of Hebe's prevarication. He strode forcefully across his office to flick the covering from the painting displayed there, his piercing gaze never leaving Hebe's face as he did so. He wanted to see her reaction to the portrait.

Her eyes widened as she stared blankly at the portrait, her body tensing rigidly.

Not surprising, really, Nick thought with hard amusement.

The painting was of her. Sitting sideways on a chair, wearing a clinging dress of midnight-blue, her hair a glorious curtain of silver down the long length of her spine.

And that was where the formality of the portrait began and ended!

Because her expression could only be called sultry, with a knowing smile curving those pouting, kissable lips, and her eyes, those wonderful golden eyes, half closed as if in arousal. Her breasts were thrust slightly forward beneath the blue dress, the material clinging so closely to those long silken limbs that it was impossible to believe she wore anything beneath it.

That *Hebe* wore anything beneath it.

Because the woman was most certainly her.

Nick had kissed those same lips six weeks ago. Seen that arousal in her eyes. Caressed the proud tilt of those breasts. Suckled on those rosy nipples. And those long silken limbs had been wrapped around him more than once that night too.

'Who is she…?'

Nick turned sharply back to look at Hebe as she spoke in a whisper, his frown deepening as he saw how pale she was, her eyes like golden orbs in that pallor.

But they both knew her question was totally unnecessary. 'Oh, come on, Hebe.' He sighed his impatience as he moved to stand beside her. 'It's *you,* damn it!' He would have reached out and shaken her, except that she looked as if she might disintegrate at the slightest touch.

No doubt she had never thought this portrait—a portrait painted by a man who had obviously put the love he felt for its subject into every brushstroke—would ever be seen by the general public. That was the reason for her obvious shock. In fact, it was pure luck that it hadn't gone into a local auction with a lot of other things from a house cleared out by relatives after the death of its owner, consequently disappearing back into the realms of obscurity.

Luckily enough, the autioneer had been experienced enough to know the Andrew Southern signature—a swan with the single letter S beside it—and had called a friend of his in London to see if any of the big dealers were interested in coming to look at it. Nick most certainly had been, getting the man's promise that he would let no one else view it until he had flown in from New York to see it.

One look at the painting, at the almost luminous style that marked it as Southern's work and not some pale imitation, and Nick had known he had to have the painting. At any price.

It had taken some time and considerable skill to negotiate that price with the new owner and the auctioneer before bringing his prize back to London this morning, and his first priority had been to talk to Hebe Johnson.

Undoubtedly the woman in the portrait.

And, at the time of the painting, Andrew Southern's lover. Something she seemed to be denying most strongly!

Hebe moved forward as if in a dream, her hand moving up to touch the painting, her fingers stopping only centimetres away from the canvas, trembling slightly. Her breathing was shallow.

'Who is she?' she repeated emotionally.

Nick stepped forward. 'For God's sake, Hebe, it's *you*—'

'It *isn't* me!' She turned to look at him, able to feel the rapid beat of her pulse in her throat. 'Look at it again, Nick,' she told him shakily, pleadingly, turning to look at the painting, a gut-wrenching pain in her chest as she did so.

'Of course it's you—'

'No,' she cut in quietly again. 'She has a birthmark, Nick. Look. There.' She pointed to the rose-shaped birthmark on the swell of one creamy breast, visible above the low neckline of the deep blue dress. 'And look here.' She pulled aside the open neck of her cream blouse, revealing her own creamy breast.

Completely bare of that rose-shaped birthmark…

Whoever the woman in the portrait was it most certainly wasn't Hebe.

She knew it wasn't.

But if it wasn't her, who—?

No, it couldn't be!

Could it…?

And that was when everything went dark…

CHAPTER THREE

NICK inwardly cursed as he leapt forward to catch Hebe before she hit the carpeted floor, swinging her up in his arms to carry her over to the leather sofa at the back of the room.

He had been expecting some sort of reaction to the portrait, but it certainly hadn't been this!

Embarrassment, perhaps—because it was obvious that Andrew Southern had been Hebe's lover. And surprise that Nick actually had possession of the portrait had also been a possibility.

But he certainly hadn't expected Hebe to faint as she denied she was the woman in the portrait!

That birthmark apart—a pretty rose-shaped mark— there was no one else it could be but her.

He laid her down on the sofa, and Hebe started to groan slightly as she came back to consciousness, finally opening her eyes to look up at him as he bent over him.

And instantly closing them again, as if even the sight of him was too much for her.

'Hey, come on, Hebe. I realise *I'm* no oil painting, but I'm not that bad either!' he mocked as he moved back slightly.

The painting, Hebe remembered with a pained wince,

trying to collect herself. But to come to terms with the enormity of what she had seen, and what she was thinking, was going to take longer than the few seconds she'd had so far.

She swallowed hard, not sure how she felt about any of this. If that portrait really was who she thought it was, then—

'Here.'

She opened her eyes to find Nick holding out a glass of water.

She was freaking him out with this 'dying swan' routine, Nick decided impatiently as he put the rest of the bottle of water back in the fridge neatly disguised as an oak filing cabinet.

Who really fainted nowadays? People who were ill, hungry or had been hit over the head! He could rule out the former, because Hebe certainly wasn't ill. Nor had she been hit over the head. Except maybe metaphorically. That just left hungry.

'Have you had any lunch today?' he prompted suspiciously.

'Actually—' she swung her legs to the floor to sit up and take a sip of the chilled water '—no.'

He gave a shake of his head as he moved back to the fridge. 'Why haven't you?' he demanded as he took a chocolate bar out and handed it to her. 'Eat it,' he instructed, when she just looked at it. 'You'll feel better if you do.'

Hebe somehow doubted that, but the chocolate certainly couldn't do any harm. She had heard it was good for shock too. And she was certainly in shock.

She glanced at the portrait again as she slowly ate two squares of the chocolate.

The woman in the portrait was beautiful, much more so

than her. Couldn't Nick see that? And that woman had a sultry air about her, a sensuality, those golden eyes half closed with a secret that only she possessed.

Hebe felt herself begin to shake again as she took an educated guess at what that secret was.

She ate another two squares of chocolate before speaking huskily. 'Where did you get it?'

'I told you—the north of England.' Nick moved restlessly about the confines of the office.

Hebe gave him an impatient glance. 'Can't you be more specific? Who did you buy it from? Where did *they* get it?' It was suddenly imperative she knew these things.

Nick raised dark brows at her intensity. 'I bought it from a young couple who had just inherited an old house from the guy's great-uncle, or something like that. They had never seen the painting before he died, because the old man had the portrait hung in his bedroom, of all things,' he revealed, with a certain amount of distaste.

He couldn't say he felt exactly comfortable with some old man drooling over a portrait of a woman—Hebe!— who was certainly young enough to be his daughter, if not his granddaughter.

But the couple hadn't known anything about the woman in the portrait—who she was or how the great-uncle had come to have her portrait. Nick had known who she was— he just didn't have any idea what her portrait was doing in some old guy's bedroom and not in the possession of the man who had painted it with such love.

Hebe didn't look as if she were about to answer that question for him now, either!

She moistened dry lips. 'What was the man's name?'

'Hell, Hebe, what difference does it make what his name

was?' Nick snapped his impatience. 'He had your portrait, isn't that enough?'

'No.' She shook her head slowly, turning to look at him with dark gold eyes. 'Because, no matter what you might think to the contrary, Nick, the woman in the portrait isn't me.' She gave a humourless smile at his obvious scepticism. 'No, Nick, it isn't,' she insisted. 'Andrew Southern couldn't possibly have painted my portrait because I've never met him! But it looks as if my mother may have done,' she added, so softly Nick had trouble hearing her.

Her mother?

Hebe was trying to say the woman in the portrait was her *mother*?

How stupid did she think he was? Of *course* the portrait was of Hebe. It couldn't be anyone else.

Could it...?

Nick gave her a dark frown. 'You're telling me that you look exactly like your mother did at that age?'

'Ah.' She gave a grimace. 'Now, *that* is a very difficult question for me to answer—'

'Why is it, damn it?' he interrupted irritably. 'How difficult can it be to know whether you do or do not look like your mother?'

Hebe eyed him ruefully, understanding his incredulity at the situation, sympathising with it, even, but at the same time knowing she didn't have the answers that he wanted.

Except for one...

She raised silver-blonde brows. 'How about if you're adopted?'

Nick stopped pacing the room, looking down at her with disbelieving eyes. Was she seriously trying to tell him, expecting him to believe—?

But why not?

Hundreds of kids were adopted every year.

He moved to stand in front of the portrait, studying it closely. He had quickly seen the mirror-like similarities, but now he looked for the differences.

There was that birthmark, of course. But that didn't prove anything. It was a pretty birthmark, and perhaps Andrew Southern had used a little poetic licence—a lover's rose-coloured glasses—when he'd painted it there above the woman's breast?

There was that air of sensuality, too, he supposed. But, God knew, he knew just how sensual and sexual Hebe was. He'd seen her look just like that the night they'd spent making love together. No, that proved nothing.

Neither did the lean length of her body, those thrusting breasts and delicately arched throat.

The ring!

There was an emerald and diamond ring on the third finger of the woman's left hand. Nick assumed that it wasn't Andrew Southern Hebe had been engaged to, but the now deceased owner of the painting. Why else would someone have kept a piece of art worth so much? Especially if keeping it had been to spite his future wife and her lover. Hebe didn't wear a ring like that anymore. But if Hebe's fiancé had realised that she was having an affair with Andrew Southern—and how could he not, with the evidence of the portrait in front of him?—then he would have had every right to break off the engagement; apart from the fact that she was wearing such a revealing dress, Hebe looked as if she had just come from her lover's arms. And Nick, better than most, knew exactly how she looked at *that* moment!

No, there was nothing about this portrait that said Hebe was telling him the truth.

But what reason would she have to lie?

Because she had been found out?

Because, having already let two wealthy men slip through her grasp, she still hoped the two of *them* might have some sort of relationship?

His mouth twisted derisively as he turned back to her. 'It's an interesting idea, Hebe, but not very plausible, is it?' he dismissed.

She straightened defensively. 'Why isn't it?'

Damn it, why couldn't she just let it go? Admit she was the woman in the portrait and tell him where the hell he could find and speak to Andrew Southern?

He shook his head. 'Because it's too damned convenient, that's why,' he snapped.

'For whom?' she challenged shakily. Because it certainly wasn't convenient for her.

Her parents had told her long ago that she was adopted, of course. They were such wonderful parents, and because of this, and the fact that she never, ever wanted to hurt them, she had never even attempted to find out who her real parents were.

What would have been the point? Obviously they hadn't wanted her when she was born, so why should they want to know about her as an adult…?

'Look, Hebe, I don't give a damn if you've posed nude for the guy. I just want a way in to Andrew Southern, past his guard-dog of an agent!' Nick told her with brutal honesty.

Hebe flinched slightly at his callousness. 'Well, when you find it,' she said evenly, 'please let me know—because after this I would like to talk to him too!'

Nick's mouth twisted derisively. 'You're right; talking isn't something you do too much of when you're in bed, is it?'

'Insults are going to get us nowhere, Nick,' she told him shakily, the chocolate seeming to have done very little to allay her shock. In fact, she felt decidedly sick now.

But then, it wasn't every day you were confronted with a painting possibly of the mother you had never known. A painting, moreover, that was everything Nick said it was.

Whoever the woman was, Andrew Southern had been in love with her when he'd painted her portrait. It was there in every brushstroke, every soft nuance of the woman's sensual beauty.

Did that mean that the artist was Hebe's father…?

Or had that been the man who had owned the portrait all these years and kept it hidden from view?

They were questions that Hebe certainly wanted answers to.

But for the moment she had to deal with Nick's disbelief…

She drew in a deep breath. 'You can think what you like about the portrait, Nick. Your opinion is really of little interest to me. *I* know that woman isn't me, and that's what's important.'

He looked at her frustratedly for several seconds. 'You're seriously expecting me to believe, if that portrait is of your mother, that it's—what?—twenty-six, twenty-seven years old?'

She shrugged at his scepticism. 'That timescale would certainly fit in with the period when Andrew Southern was still painting portraits, yes. And for the record, Nick,' she added ruefully, 'I'm not *expecting* you to believe anything. I told you, it's what *I* think that's important.'

And what she thought was that she had to see Andrew Southern herself, and ask him about the woman in the portrait…

But if a man like Nick Cavendish, with all of the prestige of the Cavendish Galleries behind him, couldn't get past the reclusive artist's agent, then how did *she* expect to do so?

She would find a way.

She had to!

There was no way she could just leave here and pretend she had never seen that portrait. The portrait of the woman who surely had to be her mother…

She would need to speak to her parents too, of course. She couldn't just go off in search of her real parents without telling them about it first. She owed them that, and they would understand, she was sure. They had brought her up with a sure sense of how important she was to them, of how much she was loved, but at the same time had taught her independence of spirit and mind. They couldn't fail to support her in her search for the woman in the portrait.

'Well, if that's all, Nick, I think I'll go now.' Hebe put the glass of water down on the low table in front of her before standing up.

And instantly swayed dizzily again.

In fact, she felt as if she really were going to be sick!

'What the hell is wrong with you?' Nick stepped forward to grasp her arm, his expression dark and brooding.

She looked up at him with slightly unfocusing eyes. 'I told you—I haven't had any lunch today.' She tried to move away from him. Even that light touch on her arm was enough to send a thrill of awareness coursing through her veins.

So much for hating him!

Reasonably she might do so; he had been nothing but

insulting today, with none of that exciting lover of six weeks ago about him. But emotionally her body still responded to his slightest touch.

'You're coming upstairs with me,' he announced grimly.

'Upstairs?' She stared at him with startled eyes.

His mouth twisted derisively. 'Don't look so worried, Hebe; I'm not so filled with lust for you that I'm dragging you upstairs to have my wicked way with you!'

'Again!' she came back tartly, stung by his mockery.

'Again,' he acknowledged tauntingly, keeping a firm hold of her arm as he walked her over to the door. 'You're dizzy from not having eaten any lunch, and I have food upstairs in my apartment; the logical thing to do is take you up there and feed you,' he explained dryly.

Logic? When had *logic* had anything to do with their relationship so far?

'If you're happy to let me go for the day, I can easily go home and get myself something to eat.' She firmly stood her ground.

She did not want to go upstairs to his apartment. Today had been humiliating enough without returning to the scene of her naïve stupidity in thinking this man seriously liked her!

Nick's mouth tightened. 'No, I'm not happy to do that, Hebe. For one thing, you don't look as if you could make it downstairs, let alone home,' he derided. 'And, for another, I haven't finished talking to you yet.'

That sounded ominous...

'I've told you—I don't know anything about Andrew Southern,' she insisted stubbornly. 'Not where he is or how you might get to meet him. I wish I did!'

Nick eyed her frowningly. Did she seriously expect him to believe that?

Yes, he acknowledged impatiently after a glance at her guileless expression, that was exactly what she expected.

It was up to him to ensure that she knew she hadn't succeeded in convincing him of anything. Not for a moment!

'We'll talk again after you've eaten,' he told her firmly, taking her with him out into the carpeted hallway.

Hebe glared at him. 'Do you never take no for an answer?'

Nick gave a wolfish grin. 'You, of all people, should know that I don't!'

That had certainly silenced her, he noted with satisfaction. That poutingly kissable mouth was set firmly as the two of them got into the private lift to go up one floor to his apartment.

Meaning that Hebe would enter his completely private domain for a second time!

'Is an omelette okay with you?' he rasped tersely, releasing her arm to stride through to the open-plan kitchen with its white and chrome fixtures.

Hebe took her time following him, obviously no more comfortable being back here than he was to have her here.

He would feed her the omelette, get some straight answers out of her, and then she could leave—

Where the hell was she?

He strode back out into the sitting room, coming to an abrupt halt as he saw her holding and looking at one of the photographs that usually stood on the coffee table in front of the window. 'What do you think you're doing?' he bit out coldly, his face devoid of all expression.

Hebe almost dropped the photograph she had picked up to have a better look at, grasping it with both hands against her chest, knowing from the furious look on Nick's face that his question didn't require an answer—that he knew exactly what she had been doing.

The photograph was of a little boy about three or four years old. A gorgeous little boy grinning happily into the camera lens. A little boy, with Nick's dark hair and blue eyes…

Nick moved forcefully across the room to snatch the photograph out of her hands, those blue eyes glacially cold as he glared at her through narrowed lids.

She swallowed hard. 'I'm sorry. I—he's very beautiful.'

A nerve pulsed in his tightly clenched jaw. 'Yes, he was,' he ground out harshly.

Was. It was his son, then.

Hebe felt a tightening of her chest at the thought of all that life and boyish happiness no longer existing.

How much worse was that realisation for Nick…!

'I'm sorry,' she said again.

Nick put the photograph carefully back on the table before giving her a sharp glance. 'You know who he is?'

'I—yes,' she admitted reluctantly. 'One of the other girls told me that you had a son.'

'Luke,' he bit out harshly. 'His name was Luke.'

Luke… Four years old. His death simply too much for his parents to deal with together, driving them irrevocably apart.

'I really am sorry,' Hebe repeated huskily. 'I shouldn't have— Please believe me when I tell you I never meant to—'

'To what?' he challenged with a lift of that arrogant jaw. 'Pry? Stick your nose in where it doesn't belong?' He gave a disgusted shake of his head, his face set in grim lines.

Hebe flinched at his obvious fury. 'It wasn't like that,' she protested softly. 'I just saw his photograph, and—' And what? Hadn't she been prying, after all? Well…yes. But not with any intention of annoying or upsetting Nick. She had just been curious, that was all.

And in being so she had turned Nick's undoubted anger on her once again.

So what was new?

But surely he knew she hadn't *deliberately* set out to cause him pain in this way? Even though it seemed that was exactly what she had done.

'I really am sorry,' she said again firmly, before moving past him to walk into the kitchen, feeling it best to give him a few minutes' privacy.

It seemed to be an afternoon for upsets. Nick where his son was concerned and her own puzzlement and curiosity about the woman in the portrait and the man who had painted it.

But *she* would possibly be able to find answers to her own questions, whereas Nick would probably never understand why his son, a little boy of four, had had to die.

It probably all came down to a matter of faith. And the death of a four year old child certainly tested that to the limits!

She looked up nervously a few minutes later as Nick came back into the kitchen, thankfully with some of the colour back in his cheeks, his expression less grim.

'I got eggs and milk out of the fridge.' She shrugged, pointing to where she had placed them on the worktop. 'I wasn't sure what else you needed.'

Nick slipped off the jacket of his suit and hung it on the back of one of the bar stools before taking down one of the frying pans from a display of them hanging from a rack above the work table in the middle of the kitchen. 'Cheese or mushrooms?' he bit out economically as he cracked the eggs into a bowl.

Hebe had to swallow down the nausea at the thought of either filling. 'Plain, if that's okay?' It still felt decidedly strange to be up here in Nick's apartment again, let alone having him cook for her.

Kate, having witnessed their departure, was going to be more than a little curious when Hebe finally returned downstairs to the gallery!

Nick's impatience was all inward as he warmed the oil in the pan while beating the eggs, before adding the milk. He was regretting now that he had made the offer to cook for Hebe in the first place.

He never talked to anyone about Luke. He couldn't. Still, three years later, he found his son's death too painful to discuss with any degree of emotional normality. It was because the subject had been too painful that he and his now ex-wife Sally had stopped talking to each other— neither of them able to think of anything else when they were together, but unable to put those thoughts into words, the whole thing being just too painful.

So he certainly didn't intend discussing Luke with Hebe, a woman he had spent a single night of passion with!

He dropped the egg mixture into the frying pan and let it cook before turning to speak to Hebe. 'You'll find a knife and fork— What the hell—!' he rasped, as a white-faced Hebe ran past him out of the kitchen, her hand pressed tightly to her mouth.

She barely made it to the bathroom that adjoined the master bedroom—ironically, the only bathroom she knew the location of—before she was well and truly sick.

It had been the smell of the eggs cooking in the frying pan that had done it, tipping her sensitive stomach over the edge, the nausea just too much to control any longer.

'Here you go,' Nick murmured behind her seconds later, and he placed a damp cloth on her forehead.

This was so humiliating!

Not quite as bad as that morning six weeks ago when, the night over, Nick hadn't been able to wait for her to leave, but pretty close.

She sat back on her heels, holding the cloth to her forehead herself now, the nausea seeming to have passed. Although quite what she had found to be sick with, considering she hadn't eaten anything today except the chocolate Nick had insisted on giving her a short time ago, was a mystery!

'Feeling better now?' Nick prompted abruptly.

'A little—thank you.' She nodded, not quite able to look at him.

She had caused nothing but trouble this morning—trouble she was sure Nick couldn't wait to be rid of.

'I'll just give my face a wash, and then I think I would like to leave, after all.' She could probably quite happily eat the omelette now that she had got rid of whatever had upset her stomach, but in the circumstances it was probably better if she didn't stay.

'I don't think so, Hebe.'

She looked up at him sharply. Only to find him staring at her with cold, glittering blue eyes, his hands clenched into fists at his sides.

'What do you mean?' she prompted warily.

'I mean I don't think that you're going to be leaving here any time soon,' Nick bit out tautly.

Hebe's eyes widened. 'But I can assure you that I feel absolutely fine now.'

'Yes, I'm sure you do,' he ground out harshly. 'It's a

curious fact, but women in your condition usually *do* feel better once they've actually been sick,' he added forcefully.

She blinked frowningly. 'My condition?'

Nick drew in a harsh breath, looking at her as if he would dearly like to put his hands around her throat and strangle her. 'Hebe, unless I'm very much mistaken—and Lord knows I hope I am!' he muttered grimly, 'the fact that you fainted a short time ago for no reason—'

'I had just seen a portrait of the mother I've never known!' she defended incredulously.

Nick shook his head, so tense Hebe almost felt as if she could reach out and touch it. 'The fact that you fainted, coupled with your earlier dizziness and your nausea just now, when I started cooking the eggs, all point to one conclusion as far as I can see.'

Hebe blinked, her hand on the side of the sink as she slowly stood up to face him. 'They do…?'

The glittering gaze moved down the length of her body, coming to rest on her stomach. 'You're pregnant, Hebe,' he bit out abruptly. 'About six weeks, I would say!' he added with barely suppressed fury.

Pregnant!

But she couldn't be!

Could she…?

CHAPTER FOUR

HE had completely forgotten, Nick realised self-disgust-edly, the *fourth* reason that women at least sometimes fainted.

Sally, when she'd been expecting Luke, had fainted several times during the early months of her pregnancy. She had woken up feeling sick every morning for the first three months, too—usually making a miraculous recovery once she had actually been sick, and so able to enjoy the rest of the day.

Hebe Johnson, Nick was pretty sure, was pregnant with his baby.

'I assumed you were on the Pill, for God's sake!' he muttered impatiently. But assumption, he knew, was the mother of all—

'What?' Hebe returned vaguely, appearing to be com-pletely dazed, her face once again deathly pale, her eyes huge luminous golden globes.

'Look, let's get out of this bathroom, at least,' he sug-gested impatiently, sure that it couldn't be helping her nausea to still be in the room where she had actually been sick. Taking a firm hold of her arm, he led her through to his bedroom when she made no effort to move herself. He sat her firmly down in the bedroom chair. 'Now,' he muttered sharply. 'I asked if you're on the Pill?'

She blinked up at him, really looking as if she were in shock this time. 'Why would I be?' she finally answered distractedly.

'For God's sake, pull yourself together, Hebe,' he snapped, and he moved away impatiently, sure that his looming over her couldn't be helping the situation.

Although if she really was pregnant he couldn't see that there was any help for either of them!

'It's quite simple, Hebe. Were you, or were you not using any contraception when we went to bed together six weeks ago?' He bit the words out as succinctly as he could in the circumstances, knowing that one of them, at least, had to try and make sense of all this.

Even if he didn't *feel* very sensible!

He had needed to be with someone that night six weeks ago—had needed to lose himself in her, to blot out the painful memories and then move on. But if Hebe really was pregnant from that night then moving on wasn't an option. For either of them…

Hebe drew in a deep breath, at last managing to fight down the panic his announcement had caused. Of course she wasn't pregnant. No matter what people said, all those dire warnings parents gave to pubescent offspring about it 'only taking once', she could not be pregnant from that single night she had spent in Nick's arms.

But it hadn't just been 'once', a little voice inside her head reminded her. She and Nick had made love three times that night. Not once.

She was *not* pregnant!

It was ridiculous to even suggest that she was.

She straightened in the chair, determined to take some control of this situation. 'No, I wasn't. But that doesn't mean—'

'Why weren't you?' Nick rounded on her impatiently. 'You're what? Twenty-five, twenty-six years old—?'

'Twenty-six,' she confirmed, her own impatience rising to meet his as she glared at him. 'But I'm not in a relationship. And I certainly don't take contraceptive pills just on the off-chance I might meet a man I want to go to bed with!'

'But that's exactly what you did!' he came back exasperatedly.

She paled even more. 'But it wasn't planned—'

'Wasn't it?' he challenged coldly. 'I seem to remember it was *you* who bumped into me that evening…'

Hebe became very still, her breathing shallow as she stared at him, her blood seeming to have turned to ice in her veins. 'And just what is *that* supposed to mean?' she prompted slowly.

He shook his head. 'You wouldn't be the first woman to set this sort of trap for a man. What were you hoping for, Hebe? That I would pay you off—'

'How dare you?' she finally managed to gasp disbelievingly.

He couldn't really think—believe— He did, she acknowledged dazedly as she saw the glittering anger in his eyes.

'Give it up, Hebe,' he bit out disgustedly. 'The outraged virgin act doesn't suit you at all!'

No, she hadn't been a virgin when they went to bed together. She had had one previous relationship before Nick. But that had been five years ago, with a fellow student at university and the experience had not been repeated until that impetuous night with Nick. Nor since, either!

She really had been totally besotted with him, had found his attention flattering, his obvious desire for her to spend the night with him too tempting to resist.

She looked at him coldly. 'Why are you turning all this round on me? I didn't notice *you* using any protection that night either!' she challenged.

He eyed her scornfully. He knew she had a point, but he was in no mood to admit that right now. 'Because no one told me I needed to!'

'Because I didn't even *think* about getting pregnant!' she snapped, standing up impatiently. 'And I'm not! This conversation is acedemic,' she dismissed. 'I'm not pregnant. I've obviously just eaten something that's dis-agreed with me—'

'You haven't eaten anything at all since yesterday,' Nick reminded her impatiently.

Well, that was true. But it still didn't mean— She could not be pregnant!

'There's one quick and easy way to settle all this,' Nick decided brusquely, marching out of the bedroom.

Hebe quickly followed him, wondering what he was going to do. He was in the kitchen, putting his jacket back on when she got found him. 'Where are you going?' She frowned her confusion; *she* was the one who was leaving, not him!

He gave her a scathing glance. 'To a chemist. To buy a pregnancy test. I don't see any point in continuing our present conversation until we know one way or the other whether you actually *are* pregnant,' he added grimly, picking up what appeared to be his car keys.

Hebe gave a firm shake of her head. 'I won't be here when you get back.'

Nick halted in the doorway, his face set into grimly determined lines as he turned back to her. 'You had damn well better be,' he warned angrily.

Hebe's chin rose challengingly. 'Aren't you afraid of what else I might "pry" into while you're gone?' she taunted.

Nick gave a humourless smile. 'Touch anything and I promise you you'll regret it,' he warned softly.

She believed him!

She believed his threat about her leaving too. But that didn't stop her, as soon as she knew he had definitely gone, from quietly letting herself out of the apartment and making her way back downstairs, pausing only long enough to pick up her jacket and bag from the staffroom before leaving the gallery.

Nick really could just go ahead and sack her if he liked!

He might be used to issuing orders and expecting them to be obeyed, but after his insults she had no intention of obeying anyone who spoke to her in that autocratic tone.

And she refused even to *think* about his assertion that she was pregnant. Of course she wasn't. The whole idea was ridiculous.

Besides, she had some telephone calls she needed to make before the close of business for the day—telephone calls she couldn't make from Nick's apartment.

She had a lot of friends from university working in the art world who, like her, had decided to work in galleries or agencies instead of painting professionally themselves. One of them, she was sure, would give her some sort of lead on Andrew Southern's agent.

She was determined to track the artist down, no matter how impossible Nick seemed to think it was. Nothing was impossible if you had the right motivation. And she most certainly had that!

Where was her mother now?

Living in England somewhere? With a husband and possibly other children?

Maybe. Hebe had no intention of disrupting her life, but now that she had seen that portrait she just needed to know.

Was Andrew Southern her father?

Why, if he had loved her mother, hadn't he married her when he knew she was expecting his child? If Hebe *was* his child…!

Why had she, Hebe, been given up for adoption?

None of those things had been of interest to her before she saw that portrait—and, whether he realised it or not, she had Nick Cavendish to thank for that!

It took half a dozen telephone calls once she got home to even track down Andrew Southern's agent, and then a call to the agency only resulted in the receptionist telling her that she could make an appointment to speak to Mr Gillespie, and he would be happy to pass along any commission she might care to make, but she very much doubted he would be able to help Hebe in regard to meeting or talking to Andrew Southern personally.

Hebe made an appointment for the following day, anyway. If nothing else she could give the agent a letter, possibly a photograph of herself, to forward on to the reclusive artist. If her mother had meant anything to Andrew Southern at all—and that portrait seemed to say that she had—then the photograph of Hebe alone would surely be enough to pique his interest!

It was what she was hoping for, at least…

* * *

Nick banged forcefully on the apartment door, his anger not having diminished in the least on the drive over here after discovering that Hebe had indeed gone from his own apartment before he'd returned.

What did she think she was playing at?

He had told her to stay put.

She hadn't.

He had told her they would talk further when he got back.

She hadn't been there to talk to.

And he was furious. With her. With himself. With the fact that he had become more and more convinced since leaving her earlier that she *was* pregnant.

If Hebe was to be believed about having had no other relationships in her life—and her anger at the suggestion had seemed fairly convincing—then he was going to have baby…

A little girl who would look like Hebe. Or a little boy who looked like him. And Luke…

He banged on the door again, his fist raised a third time when the it suddenly opened. Hebe eyed him coldly from just inside her apartment.

'There's no need to break the door down, Nick,' she snapped. 'I was just eating a sandwich when I heard your— knock,' she drawled pointedly.

He drew in an impatient breath. 'What sort of sandwich?' he demanded to know. 'You do realise that there are certain things you can't eat when you're pregnant?' he added impatiently as he walked past her into the apartment, to look around him curiously.

The apartment took up the second floor of one of the old Victorian buildings London was so famous for, with huge bay windows that looked out on a tree-lined avenue.

The sitting room was bright and sunny, the walls painted yellow, multicoloured scatter rugs on the polished wood floor, the brown sofa and chairs festooned with an assortment of cushions in autumn colours.

He turned to look at Hebe. She certainly looked a lot better than she had when he'd left her earlier. The colour was back in her cheeks, the sparkle—anger—was back in those gold-coloured eyes. She was looking very slim too, in the faded denims and fitted black tee shirt she had changed into since returning home.

Well, the slimness was soon going to change, if his assumption proved correct!

Although he had a feeling Hebe was going to be one of those women who put hardly any weight on while pregnant, and that despite the growing baby she would retain that air of delicacy that so appealed to him.

He took a crushed paper bag out of his jacket pocket. 'For you,' he told her dryly.

Hebe made no effort to take the bag from him, and in fact put both her hands behind her back instead. She knew exactly what was in the bag, and had no intention of satisfying his curiosity. 'I don't remember inviting you inside,' she said irritably.

'You didn't,' he confirmed, strolling over to where her plate, with its half-eaten sandwich, still sat on the table. He lifted one corner of the bread to look at the filling. 'Cheese.' He nodded approvingly. 'You'll need to keep up your calcium intake.'

'Nick—'

'Hebe?' he came back challengingly.

'Don't you think you've taken this far enough?' She sighed wearily, sitting down on the chair at the table.

'Insulted me enough? I told you—I was faint and dizzy from hunger earlier, and for no other reason,' she said firmly.

He put the bag down on the table next to her sandwich. 'We'll know in a few minutes, won't we?' he said grimly. 'You can do this test any time of the day and get a correct result,' he assured her determinedly.

'A negative one, you mean?' She nodded.

'Hebe.' Nick moved down on his haunches beside the chair. 'You weren't on the Pill. I didn't use any precautions, either. Did you go to the doctor for a morning-after pill?'

'Certainly not!' She was horrified at the suggestion.

'No, I thought not,' he accepted flatly. 'Have you had a period since we were together?'

Her cheeks suffused with embarrassed colour. 'Now, look—'

'Have you?' he persisted.

Had she? Her periods had never been particularly regular, anyway—sporadic at best—so she tended not to take too much notice of dates, just dealing with them when they arrived. But, no, she didn't think she had—

She grabbed the bag containing the pregnancy test, got up and strode determinedly from the room. She would do his test, prove to Nick once and for all that she was not pregnant, and then hopefully he would just go away and leave her alone.

Blue.

The little line in the middle of the window was blue.

Blue for *positive*.

Hebe sat on the side of the bath, her head bent down between her knees as she breathed in short, controlling gasps, trying not to faint again.

She hadn't believed the result the first time, had been sure it was faulty, so had taken out the second tube in the double pack—trust Nick to want to make doubly sure!—and done it again.

That one had a positive blue line through the middle of it too.

She was definitely, positively pregnant.

With Nick Cavendish's baby.

A baby *he* certainly didn't want.

Did *she*?

She had never given much thought to having a baby of her own. Or, at least, if she had, it had been as part of and a progression of a loving marriage.

Not the result of a single night spent in Nick Cavendish's arms!

Now what did she do?

She was pregnant. She had the spark of a tiny new life growing inside her. Her very own son or daughter. But it wasn't just hers. It was Nick's son or daughter, too!

And therein lay the problem. It was obvious from what Nick had said earlier that he believed she had deliberately got herself pregnant in order to trap him in some way.

What—?

'Hebe? Are you okay?' A soft knock on the bathroom door accompanied Nick's pressing query.

She straightened and looked apprehensively at the door, wondering how she was supposed to go out there and tell Nick that she was expecting his baby after all.

She could lie, of course. That was always an option. She could tell him that the result was negative—

But he wouldn't believe her, and would no doubt insist on being present when he made her do yet another test!

Because he *knew,* somehow he already knew, that she was pregnant.

'Hebe?' he prompted more urgently.

She drew in a deep breath, chewing her top lip before answering him. 'Go away,' she finally managed to groan.

There was silence on the other side of the door for several seconds, and then Nick rattled the door handle impatiently. 'Open the door, Hebe,' he ordered steadily.

'I said go away!' she muttered.

'No way,' he answered determinedly. 'Either you open the damned door, Hebe, or you stand back out of the way while I kick it down,' he instructed evenly.

He was going to kick the bathroom door down? She moved out of the way, just in case.

'That's harassment, Nick,' she told him frowningly.

'Your choice.' The shrug could be heard in his voice.

'I'm pregnant—okay!' she shouted through the locked door. 'You were right all the time and I was wrong. Because I'm pregnant!' Her voice broke slightly as saying the words brought alive the enormity of what was happening to her.

No matter what Nick might choose to think, she was not going to ask him for help. Accepting any assistance from him after the things he had implied earlier was not an option. Although she had no idea how she was going to manage to support herself and the baby, either. Even if Nick let her keep her job at the gallery, she would only be able to work until the seventh month or so. Her parents would want to help, she felt sure. But was it fair to ask them? After all, they had adopted her and given her so much—how could she now ask them to help her in single-motherhood? That would just—

She didn't have any time for further thought or worry

as the bathroom door crashed back on its hinges, the lock having splintered away from the frame as Nick kicked it.

She stared up at him dazedly as he stood in the doorway. 'You actually broke the door down,' she murmured incredulously as she stood up to examine the damage.

He shrugged, his expression grim. 'I told you that I would if you didn't unlock it.'

Yes, but— He couldn't just go around breaking up her apartment! What was her flatmate Gina going to say, when she came home from work later and saw the damage Nick had done to the door?

'You had no right to do that.' She gasped her indignation. 'No need—'

'I had *every* need, damn it,' he grated harshly. 'You wouldn't open the door.' He shrugged unapologetically. 'I couldn't tell what you were doing in here.'

She gave a dazed shake of her head. 'It's a bathroom, Nick; what could I possibly have been doing?'

'I had no way of knowing, did I? With that door between us,' he came back hardly. 'So a word of warning, Hebe,' he added tautly. 'Don't ever put a locked door between us again!'

Hebe just continued to stare at him. Had the whole world gone mad? *Her* world, at least!

Hebe didn't want to listen to him any more. She couldn't think with him glaring at her like that. His eyes were no longer filled with the shadowy pain of the past but full of accusation now instead. And that accusation was directed at her. Because he believed she had deliberately set out to get pregnant that night they'd spent together!

She didn't even look at him as she brushed past him to go back into the sitting room. It all looked so normal, exactly as she had left it this morning, with the bright autumn colours that she and Gina had had so much fun decorating with, her pot plants in the window, the early-evening sun shining through the almost floor to ceiling windows.

Only she had changed then, for she wasn't the same person who had left the apartment early this morning to go to work as usual.

She was pregnant. With Nick Cavendish's child. And that meant her life would never be back to what she thought of as normal ever again.

'Well?' She turned back to him challengingly. 'When are you going to start accusing me again of being a gold-digger? Of deliberately getting myself pregnant so that I can get my hands on all that lovely Cavendish money? Because you *do* think that's what I've done, don't you, Nick?' she scorned disgustedly.

Nick continued to look at her through narrowed lids. Yes, as he had driven to the chemist, bought the pregnancy test and driven back to his apartment only to find her gone, that was exactly what he had thought Hebe had done.

And he still did. Nothing had changed his belief about that.

It just didn't matter any more. No, damn it, it mattered—but not to the ultimate outcome. Because Hebe was having his baby. *His* baby. And, whatever she might have thought would result from this, this child was going to be his as well as hers.

'Don't bother to answer that,' she dismissed disgustedly. 'I know that's what you think. Well, do you want to know what *I* think?' Her eyes flashed like molten gold.

Nick felt some of his own anger draining out of him as he took in all her outraged indignation. She really was a beautiful young woman. A woman who would be even more beautiful as her pregnancy developed. Nick knew from when Sally had been expecting Luke that pregnant women seemed to take on a beauty all their own, glowing from the inside rather than out.

A glowingly pregnant Hebe was going to be a sight to behold.

'Yes,' he answered briskly, moving to one of the armchairs to sit down and look up at her. 'I would be very interested to hear what you think.'

'I'll bet!' Hebe scorned. 'You don't seem to have taken too much notice of what I've had to say so far!' She looked pointedly at the shattered bathroom door.

Couldn't she see that was because he had been in shock himself? Because he couldn't believe—hadn't dared to hope—despite what he had said to the contrary, that Hebe really could be pregnant with their child.

He had loved being a father to Luke, and had been devastated when his son had died so tragically, so suddenly. He had felt totally bereft. Now, it seemed, he was to be given a second chance at fatherhood. With Hebe. He had never thought about having another child after Luke, but now the opportunity had presented itself he found he wanted this baby more than anything else in the world.

It was just going to take a little getting used to…

'I'm listening now, Hebe,' he assured her gruffly.

She would just bet he was. Waiting to hear her make demands, no doubt. To try and blackmail him out of some of the Cavendish fortune!

Well he was going to be disappointed.

She drew in a deep breath. 'This is *my* baby, Nick—'

'And mine,' he put in quietly.

'But you can't be sure of that, can you?' she taunted, pacing the room restlessly as she looked at him. 'How do you know, how can you be *sure,* I haven't been with another man in the last six weeks?' she challenged.

He didn't move, but a nerve began to pulse just below his jaw. 'Have you?'

'No, I haven't, damn you!' she denied furiously. 'But there's no way you can be sure—absolutely sure—is there?' she taunted.

He continued to look at her for several long, breathless seconds, and then he nodded. 'A doctor will be able to confirm just how pregnant you are.'

Hebe looked at him, frowning, but his expression was so inscrutable it was impossible to read any emotion behind those blue eyes. 'And you will accept that?'

His eyes narrowed on her probingly. 'If you insist we can have tests done too,' he finally murmured softly.

'If *I* insist…?' she prompted suspiciously.

'Hebe, once this baby is established as mine, that's exactly what it will be!' he grated harshly.

She gave a disbelieving shake of her head. 'Are you saying you would take this baby away from me?'

'I'm not saying that at all.' He shrugged. 'Although, obviously that will ultimately be your decision.'

'I don't understand you!' she muttered emotionally.

'It's quite simple, Hebe. If you want to get your hands on "all that lovely Cavendish money" then you will also have to accept that I come along with it,' he bit out decisively.

Hebe stopped her pacing to stare at him incredulously. 'But I don't *want* your money,' she finally burst out forcefully. 'I'm not interested in it. Or you!'

'Methinks you doth protest too much,' he taunted.

'I'm not protesting at all,' she snapped, stung by his mockery. 'I'm stating a fact.'

'A fact, Hebe, the bottom line, is I now have a responsibility to you and the baby,' he shrugged.

A responsibility? Was that what she had become?

After years of independence, of paying her own way, was that was she was going to be reduced to?

No, she wouldn't become that! No matter how difficult going it alone was going to be, she wouldn't become that…

She gave a firm shake of her head. 'I don't need or want your help, thank you,' she told him stiffly.

'Haven't you understood yet, Hebe?' Nick ground out fiercely. 'I'm not asking, I'm *telling* you how it's going to be!'

Hebe raised her head to look at him numbly. 'What do you mean?'

'Simply that I am going to marry you, Hebe,' he told her grimly. 'Just as quickly as the arrangements can be made!'

Nick was going to *marry* her?

He couldn't be serious!

CHAPTER FIVE

NICK watched Hebe's face suffuse with a look of horror as the full realisation of what he had just said hit her.

Not exactly a flattering response to a proposal of marriage!

Certainly not the response he had been expecting.

Most women he knew, in Hebe's position, would have jumped at the idea of marrying him.

Hebe just looked as if he had dealt her another insult!

Unless he was just meant to *think* she was horrified at the suggestion?

He tried to force this idea from his mind. If the two of them were to be married and have a child together, there had to be some sort of common ground for them other than the baby. It would be a disaster otherwise—their marriage just a battleground. Even if they were going to be marrying for reasons other than love.

'Oh, come on, Hebe,' he chided tauntingly. 'It won't be so bad. You won't have to work any more. You can spend as much of that Cavendish money as you like redecorating my apartments, if they don't suit.' Looking round at this apartment at its warmth and homeliness, he had a feeling that the chrome and leather décor in his own homes wouldn't be what Hebe would choose at all. 'Or we could buy a house,' he suggested, as the thought occurred to him. 'It would probably be better for the baby if it had a garden to play in—'

'Stop, Nick!' she cut in forcefully. 'Just stop! I am *not* going to marry you—'

'Oh yes, you are,' Nick assured her softly.

'No. I'm. Not,' she said firmly.

'Oh-yes-you-are,' he repeated, with restrained anger.

'No!' She shook her head decisively. 'I don't want to marry you. I don't know you! You don't know me, either!' she reasoned frustratedly. 'And what you do know you don't like!'

Nick gave a lazy smile as his gaze moved slowly over the slim contours of her body. Whether she realised it or not, her nipples were taut with tension beneath that fitted tee shirt. 'Oh, I think you'll find I like my side of the bargain just fine,' he said mockingly.

Hebe eyed him with frustration, knowing he was deliberately misunderstanding her. What he was talking about was purely physical. The two of them had undoubtedly found a compatability that single night they'd spent together, but that had nothing to do with the commitment of marrying someone, living with them every day. He was thinking only of the nights—not the days, weeks and years of living together.

'I think you'll like it just fine, too, Hebe,' he murmured throatily as he stood up to move purposefully towards her. 'Would you like me to demonstrate how much you'll like it?'

'No…' Hebe took a step back, her eyes wide as she easily guessed his intention.

She already knew that she *did* like—only too well!

Nick paid absolutely no attention to her half-hearted

protest, taking her in his arms as his head lowered and his lips claimed hers.

Oh, God…!

Hebe simply melted against him, having no defences against his marauding mouth and hands as she felt the flood of warmth between her thighs, her breasts highly sensitised against the hardness of his chest.

His mouth moved hungrily against hers, sipping and tasting, the moist warmth of his tongue moving erotically against her lips before dipping deep into the hot cavern beneath.

Burning desire ripped through her, tearing her defences apart in a single assault, and her hands clung to the strength of his shoulders as she gave in to that engulfing fire.

His mouth broke away from hers, his lips and tongue trailing heatedly down the creamy column of her throat, his hands pushing her tee shirt impatiently aside. Taking one fiery nipple into the heat of his mouth, tongue caressing, teeth gently biting, he let his hand move down between her legs, cupping her there, just that touch through denim and silk making her quiver with pleasure.

She wanted— She needed—

Nick gave her what she needed, his palm pressing against the hardened nub between her legs, pressing more firmly as his mouth moved to her other breast, drawing the nipple into his mouth, sucking deeply as his tongue moved moistly, teeth biting with the same rhythm as his hand stroked, seeming to find that hardened nub unerringly as he touched and caressed her to fever pitch.

She couldn't take any more. She felt as thought she was about to explode. She could feel the pleasure building until it couldn't be contained, finally finding her release in long, convulsing waves of pleasure so deeply felt it was almost pain.

She collapsed weakly against him as he kissed her breasts gently in the aftermath of her release, realising her hands had become entangled in the dark thickness of his hair as she held him against her.

What had she done?

Stupid question—she *knew* what she had done. She just had no idea how to continue fighting Nick after responding to him so wantonly.

Nick straightened slowly, pulling Hebe's tee shirt down as he raised his head to look at her flushed face and pleasure-dazed eyes. His own body was still hard with desire—a desire he had no intention of satisfying. It was Hebe's pleasure that was important right now, to show her what they could find together any time she wanted once they were married.

She looked at him frowningly. 'But you haven't—'

'I don't need to, Hebe,' he assured her huskily. 'That was for you. Sex may not have been part of your plan, but I dare you to deny wanting me after that,' he murmured throatily.

Wrong thing to say, Nick. So very wrong, he realized, as she tensed before moving abruptly away from him.

But he had needed to make her see just what they could have together besides the baby now growing inside her.

His baby, he acknowledged again fiercely. *His.*

And he would do anything—anything at all—to ensure that Hebe realised she was going to marry him rather than be paid off.

Even take advantage of Hebe's response to him?

Yes, if that was what it took!

Damn it, he would keep Hebe naked in bed for a month if that was what he had to do to make her see sense!

Because she *would* marry him. *Would* become his wife. The mother of his child.

Hebe shook her head, trying to clear it of the cottonwool her brain had become as Nick kissed and caressed her.

She had to think, damn it. Had to make Nick understand that no matter how she responded to him she couldn't marry him.

Which, after her arousal just now, and the way she still trembled in the aftermath of that shattering release, wasn't going to be easy to do!

She raised her chin determinedly. 'That's just sex, Nick,' she dismissed firmly.

He shrugged. 'It's a start.'

'No, it isn't.' Her voice rose heatedly. 'Marriage is for people who love each other, who want to be together for the rest of their lives—'

'Or for people who have already made a baby together,' he put in pointedly.

Hebe closed her eyes, wishing she could shut out the truth of his words as easily. They *had* made a baby together. And did she have the right to deny that child both its parents?

Yes—if they didn't love each other!

But she *did* love Nick…

It was impossible to try and tell herself differently. Her fascination for him all those months ago had blossomed into love during that night they'd spent together six weeks ago.

The same time as their child had found a place and nestled inside her body…!

If Nick had loved her in return she knew that she wouldn't have hesitated in agreeing to marry him. She would be the happiest woman in the world right now if that were true.

But it wasn't. He thought she was after his money, not his love.

And surely love on one side was just as bad as no love between them at all?

'Why does it have to be marriage?' She frowned.

He raised dark brows. 'You would rather just live with me?'

'No! I mean, of course I wouldn't,' she admitted irritably. 'I simply don't understand why you feel you have to marry me.'

His mouth quirked with black humour. 'Perhaps I make it a point of honour to marry the mothers of my children? It's certainly something I've done so far in my life!' he added derisively.

Hebe looked at him searchingly. He couldn't think this child would be a replacement for the one he had lost? Luke had been Luke. This child, whether boy or girl, could only ever be itself and no one else.

She moistened her lips with the tip of her tongue. 'I realise that losing Luke must have been devastating—'

'Do you?' Even that dark humour had gone now, and grim lines were etched beside his nose and mouth. 'Yes, it was—devastating,' he conceded slowly. 'It was also three years ago. And nothing and no one can ever change that.'

'Exactly.' She breathed her relief that he had quite literally taken the words out of her mouth. 'This baby—' *Oh, God…!* 'This baby,' she began again, 'can't replace him—'

'You think that's what I want? To *replace* him?' Nick suddenly seemed bigger and more ominous in his obvious anger.

Hebe eyed him warily, knowing she had stepped onto dangerous ground. 'Well, I—'

'You can't replace people any more than you can bring them back to life!' he ground out harshly, blue eyes glittering with emotion. 'Hebe, do you have *any* idea of the significance of that night we spent together six weeks ago?'

She grimaced. 'Well, I'm pregnant, if that's what you mean—'

'No, that *isn't* what I mean!' Nick swung away from her, his hands clenched at his sides, fury emanating from every muscle and sinew of his body. 'That day, six weeks ago, was the anniversary of Luke's death,' he told her flatly. 'Three years to the day since some maniac got in his car after consuming too much wine with his business lunch and drove straight through a crowd of afternoon shoppers on the busy streets of New York. Sally and Luke were amongst them. Sally was seriously injured and Luke— Luke was dead before the medics even got there!'

Hebe could still hear the pain and horror of that day in his voice.

Not just to lose a child, but to lose him in such an awful way.

To receive a telephone call, probably from some unknown person, telling him that his wife had been seriously injured and his son was dead.

And this baby—Hebe's baby—had been conceived on the night of the anniversary of that little boy's death...

How eerie was that? Almost as if—

No, she wouldn't think of it in that way. It was just coincidence. Or perhaps a little more than that, she conceded. Nick had probably needed a woman in his bed that night to help anaesthetize him, to keep the pain of that anniversary at bay.

And because of that need Hebe was now pregnant with his child.

She shook her head. 'Please believe me when I say I really am sorry about that. It must have been awful for you. And Sally,' she added quietly.

She had known of her own baby's existence for only minutes—had no idea if it was a boy or a girl, even—but even so she knew she would be devastated if it were taken away from her now.

'But I can't marry you, Nick.' She groaned. 'People don't marry each other any more just because the woman's pregnant—'

'Judging by the fact that you were adopted, that certainly seems to have been the case in *your* family so far, I agree!' he cut in scathingly.

Hebe gasped, staring at him disbelievingly. 'That—that was—unforgivable!'

'Yes, it was,' he acknowledged, giving a self-disgusted shake of his head. 'I apologise. But I do mean to marry you, Hebe. This child will know its mother and its father. And don't tell me we don't have to get married for that, either,' he warned grimly. 'I don't want to be some part-time father with weekend and vacation access to my own kid! I mean this child to have parents who live together—two people he or she will call Mommy and Daddy.'

'And what about what *I* want?' Hebe protested emotionally.

Nick gave her a considering look. 'You were brought up by two people who loved you, weren't you? Parents who gave you the nurturing and security that your real mother, whoever she was, obviously thought she couldn't provide?'

'Yes...' Hebe eyed him uncertainly, not quite sure where he was going with this.

'Meaning you weren't left to live alone with your

mother, possibly brought up in daycare once you were old enough to be left, so that your mother could go back to work in order to support you both, not too much money coming in on that single wage. Or alternatively with a father in the background who maybe had access to you but only took it up sporadically, breaking your heart somewhere along the way—'

'It wouldn't be like that!' Hebe could quite clearly see where he was going with this now.

'Not if I agree to keep you and the child in the lifestyle to which you wish to become accustomed, no,' he acknowledged sarcastically. 'But I'm not going to do that, Hebe. The only way in which you will have that is by marrying me,' he told her implacably. 'I intend being in this child's life every single day, Hebe,' he assured her determinedly. 'There in the morning when it wakes up, to love and care for it each and every single day. There at night to read it a bedtime story, to care for it when it's sick or upset.'

'And its mother?' she demanded. 'Once you've married me to get what you want, what are you going to *do* with me?'

His expression became less intense. 'I've already shown you what we can have together, Hebe,' he drawled mockingly. 'It's all I have to give.'

She couldn't deny her response to him. Couldn't deny his response to her—had felt his need pressed against her, as throbbingly heated as her own desire.

But would that last? More to the point, was it enough to base a marriage on?

'Has it occurred to you, Nick,' she said slowly, 'that perhaps now I know your conditions I may not even *want* this baby?'

His hands clenched at his sides, his expression grimly

forbidding. 'I hope you're not talking about what I think you are!'

Hebe sighed, knowing abortion wasn't even a possibility as far as she was concerned. That it wasn't as far as Nick was concerned either, if his sudden fury was anything to go by.

'No,' she conceded heavily. 'I couldn't do that.'

'I should damn well hope not,' he rasped uncompromisingly.

She shook her head. 'It was just an idea. Not one I meant to be taken seriously, I might add,' she said, as she saw his anger hadn't abated in the least at her explanation.

'If I thought for a moment that it was—'

'I've said that it wasn't!' she defended firmly. 'I can't even think straight at the moment, Nick.' She sighed. 'This is all just too much on top of everything else. I don't even know who I really am!' she explained shakily.

'Then we'll find out together,' he said quietly. 'In fact, I insist on it,' he added hardly.

Frowning, she looked at him. 'What do you mean?'

'Isn't it obvious, Hebe?' he rasped impatiently. 'You're expecting a baby, but you don't know for certain who your real parents were—not their medical history, anything. For the baby's sake, at least, I think we need to know those things, don't you?'

For the baby's sake...

Of course. How could she have thought Nick would offer to help her for any other reason? After all, he believed the woman in the portrait was her! And that she had deliberately got pregnant!

It was as if she had had a bucket of ice water thrown over her. The trembling of her body was for quite another reason now.

'Yes,' she acknowledged hollowly, having no intention of telling him that she had already made an appointment to speak to Andrew Southern's agent tomorrow. She would keep that appointment alone and find out what she could about the woman she thought was her mother, and her relationship with Andrew Southern.

He nodded briskly. 'The first thing we need to do concerning that is talk to your parents—see if they know anything, anything at all, about your real parents.'

'But of course they don't.' Hebe frowned. 'They would have told me if they did.'

'Would they?' Nick prompted softly.

'Of course,' she answered impatiently. 'What possible reason could they have for not telling me?'

He shrugged. 'Perhaps the fact that they wanted you to have a settled, loving childhood, and not have your life ripped in two, as some adopted children's lives seem to be once they've located their real parents.' He shook his head. 'I don't know, Hebe. But I do think we at least have to ask them, don't you?'

'I suppose so,' she agreed reluctantly. 'I'll go and see them at the weekend—'

'*We'll* go and see them at the weekend,' Nick corrected firmly. 'It's going to be *we* in everything from now on, Hebe,' he told her firmly, and she looked at him with a frown.

We.

Hebe and Nick.

Hebe and Nick Cavendish.

How unlikely was that?

Completely unlikely! There was no way she could agree to marry this man just because he said she must. Absolutely no way!

'Tomorrow I'll see what I can do about arranging for the two of us to get married as quickly as possible.' Nick nodded distractedly, obviously having taken absolutely no notice whatsoever of her refusal. 'Today is Thursday, so I think it might be better if you took the rest of the week off. Saturday we'll go and see your parents, and Sunday we'll move your things into my apartment—*our* apartment,' he corrected ruefully.

'I'm not moving into your apartment on Sunday or at any other time!' Hebe protested incredulously. 'And I'm not marrying you either!'

'Of course you are,' he answered mildly.

'No—'

'Yes, Hebe, you are,' he repeated patiently.

'Is what I want to be of absolutely no consideration at all?' she gasped.

Nick eyed her critically. 'But you *are* getting what you want, Hebe. More than you want, in fact,' he added sarcastically. 'You really hadn't planned on getting me as your husband into the bargain, had you?' he mused grimly.

If Nick had loved her, if he had wanted to marry her, then she wouldn't have hesitated to say yes to his proposal. But he had made his feelings for her all too plain: he thought she was an opportunist and a gold-digger.

'You can't force me—'

'Calm down, Hebe,' he soothed. 'All this upset isn't good for the baby.'

The baby. That was all he cared about. All he would *ever* care about...

'I will marry you, Hebe. I insist on it. Do you really think you have the right to deny our child all the things I can give it? Or do you want this to deteriorate into a battle?' he added softly. 'A battle I would have every intention of winning?'

She blinked, a sinking feeling in the base of her stomach. 'What do you mean?'

He wasn't being fair, threatening her in this way. He knew he wasn't. But marriage between them was non-negotiable as far as he was concerned. Hebe could have anything and everything she wanted as his wife—but only as his wife.

'I would fight you for custody, Hebe,' he told her flatly. 'In fact, if you persist in fighting me on this I'll go to my lawyers right now and draw up papers to set the custody battle in motion.'

She was looking at him as if he were some sort of monster now. And maybe he was. But he wouldn't back down on this. He couldn't. There was too much at stake. He couldn't let this second chance at being a father pass him by.

She swallowed hard. 'You would really do that…?'

'If I'm forced to, yes,' he bit out tautly.

'Even if it meant I'd end up hating you?' she said emotionally.

Having Hebe hate him from the onset was not a good idea, he knew, but what choice was she giving him…?

'Even then,' he said grimly.

Hebe was looking at him now as if she had never seen him before—or as if she wished she never seen him in the first place!

She shook her head, turning away. 'I think I would like to be alone now for a while, if you don't mind,' she said abruptly.

Nick did mind—was reluctant to leave her. Even for a moment. He wasn't sure, now that she knew he was insisting on marriage rather than the settlement she had hoped for, that she wouldn't attempt to run away from him and hide if he left her on her own. Unless he could convince her beforehand that there was nowhere she could go that he wouldn't find her!

'We are getting married, Hebe,' he told her softly. 'You are going to move into my apartment. And we are going to see your parents on Saturday. And don't think I wouldn't find you if you tried to run away from me,' he added challengingly, knowing by the way her cheeks paled that she had at least been thinking about doing exactly that.

Hebe looked at him with dull eyes. 'You're really serious about this?'

'Most assuredly,' he bit out.

She nodded. 'I'll call my parents and tell them to expect us some time in the afternoon,' she said.

'And you'll move into my apartment on Sunday?'

She sighed. 'Let's just take one step at a time, hmm?'

They didn't have time for 'one step at a time', damn it!

But one look at her pale and drawn face told him that she really had had enough for one day.

Maybe he shouldn't have said those things to her in her condition. They were the truth, but maybe he shouldn't have been so harsh.

Or told her about Luke…!

But he hadn't felt he could do anything else in the circumstances. He had been fighting for his life—and his baby—and if that meant he had to fight dirty, then he was willing to do it.

Maybe he shouldn't have made love to her in that way, either. She was pregnant, after all. But he hadn't, as she chose to think, just wanted to prove a point to her. He had needed to hold her, to make love to her, and he knew he had been needing to do so ever since he'd seen her again in the gallery earlier this afternoon, his body responding uncontrollably just at the sight of her.

Even before that…!

He had tried to put her from his mind these last six weeks, in the same way he had every other woman he had been involved with since he and Sally parted, but Hebe had persisted in popping into his mind at the most inconvenient of times.

Because she had been so delicious to make love to, he had told himself. Because she had made love to him so deliciously too.

But neither of those things explained why he had still been able to imagine the delicate curve of her cheek, the beauty of those unusual gold-coloured eyes, the way a dimple appeared in her left cheek when she smiled, the husky sound of her laugh.

And then he had seen the portrait.

A portrait he had been convinced on sight was Hebe, the woman who had been haunting his days—and nights—for the last five weeks.

He had been filled with a mindless fury the first time he'd looked at the portrait, his imagination running riot and his mind going into overdrive thinking of the scenario that might have preceded the painting of it. Hebe's face and body were exactly as they had looked that night five weeks before, when *he* had made love to her.

He had known then and there that he had to have the portrait—and that, despite it being an almost priceless Andrew Southern, once he had it no one else would be allowed to look at it but him.

He had also known in that moment that he didn't want

anyone else but him to see the real Hebe like that again, either—that he wanted to take her back to his bed and keep her there.

He hadn't expected it to happen quite in this way, but the ultimate result was the same. And this way he didn't have to admit to any of these feelings. He could take Hebe as his wife whether she wanted it or not.

For better or for worse…!

'Okay,' he conceded huskily. 'I'll call round tomorrow evening and let you know what I've managed to sort out about the wedding.' No matter what Hebe said he wasn't letting go of that; she *would* marry him. And soon. 'Maybe the two of us could go out to dinner?'

Hebe gave him a rueful smile. 'I think it's a little late for us to start dating, don't you?'

'You said it yourself, Hebe. We need to start getting to know each other,' he insisted. 'By my reckoning, we have precisely seven and a half months in which to do that!'

By her reckoning too, Hebe mused dully, feeling as if a trapdoor were closing behind her. She had no doubts whatsoever that Nick meant it when he said she wouldn't be able to hide from him and that he would find her.

He meant what he said about marrying her too.

Just as he meant his threat regarding a fight for custody of the baby she carried deep inside her if she didn't agree to marriage.

It was obvious why he felt so strongly about it too. Luke's death meant that he had no intention of losing this second child.

But by this time tomorrow she would have been to see David Gillespie, Andrew Southern's agent, and would have at least set that situation in motion.

Once she had the answers she needed she would take great delight in telling Nick just exactly how wrong about her he had been!

In regard to the portrait, at any rate…

This pregnancy she couldn't, and wouldn't, do anything about.

Which meant she either had to marry Nick or fight him.

With all the Cavendish millions behind him, it was a fight she already knew Nick was sure to win!

That trapdoor closed with a resounding bang!

CHAPTER SIX

HEBE knew she was no closer to accepting her fate, when she opened the door to Nick's knock the following evening, than she had been the previous day.

But she had taken the day off as he'd suggested—it had fitted in with her appointment to see David Gillespie, anyway. An appointment that had been as frustratingly unsatisfactory as the secretary had warned her on the telephone that it would be.

No, David Gillspie had told her. He couldn't possibly reveal Andrew Southern's address. No, he certainly couldn't give her the artist's telephone number either. No, it didn't matter that her mother was an old friend of the artist. He still couldn't give her the address or telephone number.

Hebe had even tried mentioning the portrait—also to no avail. It wasn't catalogued in the artist's work, so it was probably a fake, the elderly man had claimed regretfully.

The best that Hebe had been able to get was a promise that yes, he would forward a letter on to the artist. But with the added warning that she probably wouldn't receive a reply!

Hebe didn't agree with him, and she had taken a great

deal of time and care over the wording of that letter, including a recent photograph of herself, too.

Of course it was Friday today, so Andrew Southern wouldn't receive the letter until tomorrow at the earliest. But surely once the weekend was over the letter and photograph would elicit some sort of a response?

If it didn't, then Andrew Southern wasn't the man she'd thought he was!

'You look beautiful,' Nick told her huskily as he took in her appearance in a fitted black knee-length dress, before stepping forward to plant a light kiss on her mouth.

A kiss that took her totally by surprise!

So much so that she felt herself respond instinctively, before common sense took over and she moved abruptly away; this man was forcing her to marry him! 'There's no need for any sort of play-acting when we're alone, Nick,' she told him curtly.

'Who's play-acting?' He raised dark brows over mocking blue eyes, looking wonderfully handsome in a black silk shirt and a gunmetal grey jacket, his black fitted trousers sitting low down on narrow waist and thighs. 'I happen to enjoy kissing you. I had the distinct impression you enjoyed being kissed by me too...' he added scathingly. 'And I would have thought that when we're alone—considering what our kisses usually lead to—would be exactly the right time!'

Hebe felt a delicate blush highlight her cheeks. As he'd said, she enjoyed a lot more than being kissed by him.

'I'm merely pointing out that my flatmate has already gone out for the evening, so there's no one to impress!' she bit out dismissively.

His brows rose even higher. 'I'm beginning to wonder

if this elusive flatmate exists!' he taunted, obviously deciding to ignore her jibe.

Hebe's mouth tightened . 'Oh, she exists,' she assured him tersely. 'Are we going straight out to dinner?' She wasn't even sure she was going to be able to eat; nothing else she had eaten today seemed to have wanted to stay down.

Being pregnant, she was quickly discovering, was a very uncomfortable state to be in. In fact, at the moment it felt a little like the seasickness she had suffered as a child on a day trip to Calais with her parents!

But this was only in the early stages of pregnancy, so the magazine she had bought when she went out earlier had informed her. Perfectly normal. The sickness usually disappeared by about the fourth month.

Only another seven or eight weeks to go, then!

By which time, if she didn't manage to keep any food down at all, she would have lost weight rather than gained any!

'Yes, straight out, I think,' Nick decided lightly. 'Hopefully there will be less chance of us having an argument if we're in the middle of a crowded restaurant!' he added derisively.

Hebe arched a blonde brow. 'Do you think so?'

Nick chuckled. 'Not really, no.' His gaze sharpened. 'How are you feeling today?'

'In what way?' She avoided his question as she collected her cream silk jacket from the back of the chair where she had put it earlier, having no intention of going anywhere near her bedroom once Nick arrived.

They might never leave the apartment at all if she did that—and, no matter what Nick might think to the contrary, Gina really did exist, and was expected back later this evening!

Nick's mouth twisted wryly. 'In any way!'

'Well, I haven't changed my mind about marrying you, if that's what you mean,' she muttered, as she slipped her arms into the jacket he held out for her.

His mouth tightened now. 'Hebe, could we at least start the evening without fighting?'

She shrugged. 'You were the one who asked!'

'And we both know I was referring to your nausea,' he came back impatiently.

'Then why didn't you just say so?' She grimaced. 'I've only been sick four times today so far. Not bad, considering I haven't been able to eat or drink anything all day!'

Nick frowned at this information, not at all happy with the fact that she was being quite so sick. He had noted the paleness of her cheeks when he'd arrived, but had hoped that was just due to the tension of the situation.

'Sally—my ex-wife,' he explained shortly, 'saw a guy over here when she was pregnant with Luke. I think it might be advisable for me to make an appointment for you to go and see him—'

'No!' Hebe cut in vehemently, her expression fierce. 'I don't want to go and see some specialist your wife saw when she was expecting Luke!' He looked surprised by her forcefulness.

Nick frowned darkly. 'Why the hell not? This guy's the best that there is.'

'I'm sure he is.' She grimaced. 'But Sally was your wife, and I'm just—just—'

'The woman who is shortly going to be my wife,' he cut in grimly.

Was everything going to be this much of a battle with Hebe? Probably, he acknowledged heavily.

But he wasn't going to give up. Making sure his baby was all right and having Hebe in his bed was going to be worth every battle scar…

'Hebe, you may as well get used to the idea,' he told her firmly. 'You and I, and the baby you're expecting, are going to be a family. End of story.'

She gave him a pitying look. 'If you really think it's going to be that simple then I feel sorry for you!'

Of course he didn't think it was going to be that simple. He already knew just how determined Hebe could be, how with her it was the irresistible force meeting the immovable object; he just happened to believe that the sooner she accepted they were going to be married the better it would be for both of them!

And the baby…

The thought of Hebe pregnant with his child was still strange to him. It was a wonder, a miracle, and even if he was not at all happy with Hebe's methods he knew he had spent most of the day walking around with a ridiculous smile on his face. More than one of his exployees had done a double-take at it.

About the same amount of time Hebe had spent being thoroughly sick, by the sound of it.

'Come on.' He took a firm hold of her arm. 'We'll simply go through the menu until we find something that *does* stay down!'

Bruschetta and olives, Hebe eventually found, after a false start with soup and asparagus; the latter she hadn't even got as far as her mouth, the smell having been enough to put her off.

'Better?' Nick murmured, with obvious relief.

Obviously he wasn't used to taking out such a fastidious eater, and normally she wouldn't have been—had always been able to eat anything in the past.

But the *maître'd* at this exclusive restaurant was most attentive, seeming completely unconcerned that the waiter had had to bring three starters before they found something Hebe could eat, simply whisking away the plates that had offended.

Obviously there were some benefits to being out with Nick Cavendish, after all!

'Would you like me to order some more?' he offered, once she had eaten all the bread and succulent olives with obvious enjoyment.

Embarassingly so, if she thought about it. But she had been hungry.

She grimaced. 'Let's just wait and see if this stays down, shall we?' She frowned across at him questioningly. 'I hope that isn't a smile I see on your face?'

Nick instantly sobered. 'Not at all. I'm just pleased you've found something you can eat.'

Hebe continued to eye him suspiciously for several seconds, but as he continued to blandly meet her gaze she finally gave up. 'Believe me, pregnancy isn't all it's cracked up to be,' she muttered, disgruntled.

'Not many things are,' Nick drawled.

She stiffened defensively. 'I hope that wasn't yet another snipe at me?'

'Not at all,' he came back smoothly. 'In fact, I've left all my sniper bullets at home this evening! Did you telephone your parents today?' he prompted briskly, before she could come back with another sharp comment.

She had. And a very difficult call it had been, too. She couldn't just tell her parents over the telephone that she was pregnant, for goodness' sake; she owed them more than that.

But as soon as she had mentioned bringing a male friend home with her, her mother had gone into hyperdrive. No doubt she had the colour of the bridesmaids' dresses and the flowers picked out for the wedding already!

Which posed yet another problem for Hebe.

If, as Nick insisted, she really *did* have marry him, or risk him trying to take the baby from her, then she didn't want her parents to realise why they were getting married. She knew she wouldn't be able to keep the baby secret for long, and she didn't mind them finding out about that so much, but she couldn't let them see that Nick didn't love her.

Her parents, she was sure, had always dreamt of a romantic wedding for their only daughter—with a white flowing dress, and orange blossom, and confetti by the bucketful.

The quick wedding that Nick had talked about would no doubt be a visit to a register office with none of those things!

But even that wouldn't have been so bad if the main ingredient had been in evidence.

Love.

Like her parents, Hebe had always assumed she would marry someone she loved, who loved her in return. Fifty per cent of that—her own feelings for Nick—just wouldn't do!

'Hebe?' Nick prompted guardedly at her continued silence.

She drew in a ragged breath. 'Yes, I called them. I told them I was bringing you to meet them on Saturday. They jumped to the obvious conclusion,' she added flatly.

That she was bringing home the man she intended marrying, Nick hoped. He wondered why Hebe didn't look a little happier about it.

It was what she wanted, after all. The Cavendish money at her disposal. The fact that he came along with the money might have come as something of a shock to her, but, as he had just told her, not too many things turned out quite as you planned them!

Including the way he felt about Hebe…

When his marriage to Sally, his college sweetheart, had broken down, he had vowed never to fall in love or marry again. But inwardly he had known after that one night he and Hebe had spent together—and tried to dismiss!—that Hebe was different. He'd known and been all the crueller in dismissing her the following morning.

But he hadn't forgotten her in all the weeks he had been away. In fact he hadn't so much as looked at another woman during that time—had known then that he would have to see Hebe again when he got back to London.

Of course he hadn't expected the portrait!

Or to come back to London and find that Hebe was pregnant!

Deliberately so?

He couldn't be absolutely sure about that. That was the problem…

But at least he was willing to make a go of this marriage. Why didn't Hebe just accept that if he had decided just to go for custody of the baby when it was born she wouldn't have found herself in half such an advantageous position?

'Never mind, Hebe,' he advised hardly, reaching into his jacket pocket to take out a small velvet box and place it on the table in front of her. 'Maybe this will help cheer you up.' He sat back to watch her reaction.

Which wasn't at all what he had imagined it would be.

Hebe was staring down at the ring box as if it were about to leap up and bite her!

Or maybe it was just that she had thought she would get

to choose her engagement ring herself, he realised harshly. A nice big rock of a diamond, no doubt.

Remembering the ring inside the box, Nick didn't think she was going to be disappointed!

He was.

What idiotic part of his brain had tried to convince him to give Hebe a chance? That perhaps he had been mistaken about her motives and maybe she hadn't got herself pregnant deliberately at all?

Whichever part it was, it needed shooting!

'For God's sake open it, Hebe,' he rasped, and sat forward slightly. 'I'm pretty sure you're going to like it,' he said impatiently. 'And if you don't we can change it for something bigger and better,' he added mockingly.

He was a fool, a blind, stupid fool, for wanting to believe that maybe Hebe's physical reaction to him meant she felt something more for him, after all, than just an appreciation of his bank balance.

But she was right. It was just sex.

Well, she could have as much of that as she liked. He would keep his emotions for the baby when it was born!

Hebe swallowed hard, reaching out for the box tentatively, sure she already knew what was inside. She felt stunned by the gesture. Nick had said they were getting married. Just that. But if her hunch was right this box contained an engagement ring. It was so totally unexpected.

She looked up at him uncertainly before opening the box, searching those hard, uncompromising features for some sign that this ring meant any more than a shackle of ownership.

The narrowed coldness of his eyes, that mocking twist to his lips, told her it didn't.

She lifted the lid to the box, not quite gasping as she

gazed down at the ring inside, but her breath definitely arrested in her lungs, and her eyes were wide.

It was the hugest diamond she had ever seen—several carats at least—surrounded by half a dozen slightly smaller diamonds, and the name on the lid of the box alone told her it must have cost a small fortune. A very minute part of the Cavendish millions, but still a fortune.

She closed the lid with a resounding snap. 'Why are you giving me this?' she challenged.

'Why do you think?' he snapped impatiently.

'Are you deliberately trying to insult me?' She frowned agitatedly, pushing the box back across the table at him before putting both her hands firmly under the table, as if to stop him making her accept something she didn't want. Or need.

An engagement ring between them was a farce. And that ring—that ring with its gaudy diamonds—was nothing but an insult.

Nick made no effort to take the box. 'You would have preferred a sapphire instead, maybe? Or possibly another emerald? We can go back to the store tomorrow—'

'I don't remember saying I wanted an engagement ring from you at all,' she told him forcefully. 'But that—*that*— You *are* deliberately trying to insult me, aren't you?' She glared at him, two bright spots of angry colour in her cheeks.

His eyes glittered with a similar anger. 'What's wrong with it? Not big enough? I'm sure they have others—'

'Not big enough!' she repeated incredulously. 'If the diamonds had been any bigger they would have blinded everyone in the restaurant.'

She would *not* walk around with that thing on her finger—a deliberately ostentatious sign of ownership. She might as well walk around with a neon sign over her head saying *This woman has just been bought!*

Because that was obviously what Nick thought he had done!

'Will you keep your voice down, Hebe?' he muttered, as several other diners looked their way curiously. 'Tell me what's wrong with the ring, and we'll change it.'

She glared at him. 'If that had been a diamond an eighth, even a quarter of the size, it might—just might—have been acceptable. But that—that isn't a ring. It's a ball and chain!' She was breathing deeply in her agitation. 'I think I would like to leave now, if you don't mind.' She placed her napkin firmly back on the table.

'Fine—if that's what you want!' He threw his own napkin on the table, signalling for the bill, needing to get out of here himself.

He knew she'd said she didn't want to get married, but she didn't have to throw it back in his face quite so vehemently! Why didn't she just accept that there was no way she was going to get any of his money unless she became his wife? What *was* it about this woman?

A woman who made his pulse sing and his body rouse with desire every time he looked at her!

Hebe could feel the displeasure emanating from Nick as the two of them left the restaurant.

But what else had he expected—presenting her with that gaudily over-the-top ring?

That she would gather it up with greedy hands, no doubt, she recognised heavily.

But she had hated that ring, and all that it represented, on sight.

Couldn't Nick see that…?

'Will you be able to return the ring and get your money back?' she prompted abruptly as they approached Nick's car.

'Don't worry about it,' he dismissed tersely, opening the car door for her.

It was a beautiful, low red sports-car—the sort of car that Hebe had only ever seen in glossy magazines. The sort of car you would expect a man like Nick to drive. And this was only the car he owned and drove while in London. Goodness knew what other cars he had in Paris and New York!

'This is a nice car,' she offered placatingly once they were both safely seated inside, aware of the impending visit to her parents tomorrow, and that she hadn't spoken to Nick about it yet.

She still had to ask for his help in convincing her parents this was a love-match rather than a marriage of convenience. *Nick's* convenience!

He nodded curty. 'I'll buy you one like it, if you like.'

She drew in a sharp breath. 'And why would you want to do that?'

'Oh, cut the act, Hebe,' he told her uninterestedly. 'I'm really not convinced.'

That she wasn't after his money or the expensive gifts he was deliberately offering her...

'Fine—buy me the car,' she accepted heavily, knowing that nothing she said or did would convince this cynical man she wasn't just after his money. 'As long as you accept that in another six months you'll have to pry me out of it with a tin opener!' she muttered sarcastically.

When she was nearly eight months pregnant with their baby...

The baby that had become so real to her during her hours alone at the flat today.

Everywhere had been so quiet and peaceful, so much so that Hebe had been able to hear her own heartbeat, had imagined the tiny heartbeat inside her. She had laid her hands protectively on the flatness of her stomach and mentally tried to reach inside and talk to that flickering life.

And she had been sure she received the echoing answer—*I'm here...*

She glanced at Nick, wishing she could share that with him but knowing she couldn't—that he wouldn't understand the wonder she felt at the life growing inside her. Without being sexist, she supposed no man could completely understand the miracle of it all.

Especially when that man believed the pregnancy was only a means to an end as far as she was concerned.

'I'm sure you'll cope,' Nick dismissed impatiently, weary of every damned thing turning into an argument.

This wasn't just a battle, it was a minefield!

And Hebe obviously sensed that too, staying silent on the drive back to her apartment—a still empty apartment as they had only been gone an hour or so. She removed her jacket before eyeing him warily.

'What?' he prompted tersely, the tension finally getting to him.

She moistened her lips with the tip of her tongue before answering him.

Something Nick dearly wished she hadn't done as he found himself fascinated by the sensuality of the movement, his gaze locked on the pink edge of her tongue as it moved softly over those highly kissable lips.

Lips he desperately wanted to kiss!

At least on that level he could reach her, could understand her, and give her something they both got satisfaction from.

The type of satisfaction he had craved since he had parted from her twenty-four hours ago. Just thinking about her caused a stirring in his body, and the cold shower he had taken before coming over here earlier had done nothing to alleviate his discomfort.

But before he could take the step needed to pull her into his arms and make love to her, Hebe, unaware of his rising desire, began to answer him.

'I need to talk to you about this visit to my parents tomorrow,' she began awkwardly.

Ah. Yes. Nick could see how this was going to be a problem for her.

'No need,' he dismissed dryly. 'I take it your parents wouldn't be too happy if they knew the real reason we're getting married? That it would be—preferable if they believe we're actually in love with each other?'

Colour heightened her cheeks. 'They—they wouldn't understand this situation at all.' She grimaced.

No, he didn't for a moment think that they would understand their daughter's calculating machinations. Any more than his own parents would. Although he had no doubt that they would welcome Hebe into their family. The fact that she was expecting their grandchild would be enough to ensure that.

They would probably like Hebe for herself too, though, he admitted grudgingly. She was a warm and likeable woman apart from the fact that he didn't trust her motives at all—she might have refused the ring, but surely that was just because she didn't want to have to marry him to get her hands on his money. She certainly hadn't created such a fuss about his offer to buy her a sports-car. And once they were safely married she would no doubt be willing to accept a damn sight more than that!

Hebe was a mercenary little gold-digger, and the sooner he accepted that the better off he would be!

He shrugged. 'That isn't a problem for me, Hebe. But how do you think you'll cope with pretending to be in love with me?' he added tauntingly.

Hebe kept her lashes lowered over her eyes, her expressive golden eyes that she knew would show him at that moment that no pretence was necessary where she was concerned. In spite of everything, she *did* love Nick. To the point of distraction.

She already loved the baby growing inside her too.

And maybe, maybe after they were married, with time, Nick might even come to love her?

Or was she just living in fantasy land?

Probably, she acknowledged self-derisively. But that fantasy was all she had to cling to at this moment.

Because she was going to marry him. She now saw it as the only chance she had of showing him she wasn't the woman he thought she was.

Starting with drawing the line, a very firm line, at what gifts she would accept from him and what she wouldn't. Their baby wasn't for sale, and neither was she—and the sooner Nick realised that the better!

Her face was deliberately expressionless as she looked at him. 'I'm sure I'll cope too,' she derided. 'After all, we both know how charming you can be when you choose!' she added cuttingly, remembering exactly how charming he had been that evening six weeks ago.

Charming enough for her to believe he really was interested in her.

How naïve she had been…and she was certainly paying for that naïveté now!

'I'm very tired, Nick,' she sighed. 'If you wouldn't mind going now, I think I would like to go to bed…?' she added warily as he stared at her broodingly from across the room.

He wasn't staying here tonight, if that was what he thought. Her bedroom door was remaining shut against him until after they were married! Hopefully by then she would have convinced him of her innocence, at least.

'I don't mind at all,' he finally answered with hard dismissal. 'I didn't get to finish my dinner earlier, so I think I'll go and get myself something else to eat,' he added dryly.

Hebe gave him a sharp look, stung by his easy acquiescence to her request that he leave. 'You're going out again?'

Nick gave her a mocking look. 'Does that bother you?'

Yes! Came the instant answer. It bothered her very much.

After all, she was probably just one of several women Nick had been involved with during his visits to England. No doubt one of those other women would be quite happy to join him for a late supper. And whatever else was on offer…

Hebe realised that fidelity in their marriage was something else they hadn't discussed. The thought of Nick in bed with some other woman was totally unacceptable to her, but if she told him that he would probably laugh in her face!

'Not in the least,' she assured him dismissively.

His expression darkened ominously. 'That's what I thought,' he rasped. 'But once we're married, Hebe, get used to the idea that I will be the *only* man in your life. In your bed. Is that understood?' he prompted hardly.

She eyed him challengingly. Nick had unwittingly played right into her hands. 'And does the same apply to you?'

'Oh, yes, Hebe,' he murmured throatily as he took a step towards her, easily taking her in his arms and moulding her body to his. 'Keep me happy in your bed, and I promise I'll stay there,' he assured her throatily before his mouth claimed hers.

This wasn't quite the answer Hebe wanted to hear, but now Nick was kissing her she could no longer think straight.

She didn't have a single lucid thought in her head but her desire for him as his tongue moved tantalisingly over her lips to part them and deepen the kiss.

His hands moved up to cradle each side of her face, holding her mouth up to his as he explored with his tongue, sucking the moist warmth of her own tongue into his mouth and gently biting, arousing emotions in her that caused a pulsing warmth between her legs. Her whole body was trembling with need when he finally lifted his head to look down at her desire-drugged eyes and full, still-parted lips.

'Yes.' He murmured his satisfaction as he released her. 'I don't think pretending to be in love with you is going to be any hardship at all! Sure you still want me to leave, Hebe?' he added tauntingly.

Yes!

No…!

Of course she didn't want him to leave; she would much rather have just melted in his arms.

But the relevant word in his statement was 'pretending', and that was all being in love with her would ever be to Nick—a pretence.

'I'm sure,' she murmured huskily.

He gave a dismissive shrug. 'Your loss.'

Oh, yes, she knew that, Hebe acknowledged heavily as she watched him go, waiting until the apartment door had closed softly behind him before dropping weakly down into an armchair.

How was she going to be able to bear being married to a man she loved but who felt nothing but contempt for her?

A man who only had to touch her to melt her to the core of her being…!

CHAPTER SEVEN

'STOP looking so worried, Hebe,' Nick told her derisively as she sat beside him on the drive to her parents' home. 'Didn't I already prove last night that my performance in front of your parents will be faultless? As yours had better be when you meet *my* parents,' he added grimly.

Hebe eyed him sharply. 'I'm going to meet your parents…?' She simply hadn't given Nick's family a thought, and realised she had no idea what it consisted of, besides his ex-wife Sally and Luke.

'Well, of course you're going to meet my parents,' Nick came back impatiently. 'And the rest of the Cavendish clan eventually too, no doubt.' He gave her a brief glance. 'I thought you understood, Hebe, my main home is in New York.'

'You're expecting me to move to New York with you?' She gasped in dismay.

She had assumed England would be their main home, had never even imagined that Nick would expect her to—

But *why* hadn't she? Her wants and wishes hadn't been of too much importance so far in this relationship.

In fact, Nick seemed to be of the opinion that if he kept her 'barefoot and pregnant', and satisfied in his bed, she should just be happy with the fact that he was keeping her at all!

She didn't want to move to New York, Nick realized irritably. Yet another mistake he had made where Hebe was concerned!

'I'd have thought most women would love living in New York. But if you prefer we'll buy a house in England.' He sighed. 'It ultimately makes no difference to me where we live, I suppose.' In fact, the more he thought about it, a house out in the London suburbs, with a big garden for their child to play in as it grew up, didn't sound like such a bad idea.

She was eyeing him uncertainly. 'You would really do that…?'

'Why not?' He shrugged. 'I can travel to Paris and New York from here as easily as I can travel to London and Paris from New York.'

Of course he could, Hebe acknowledged frowningly. And if he had become bored with her in his bed by then he could also see whatever women he chose when visiting those other cities!

'Fine,' she accepted abruptly, turning to look sightlessly out of the window.

This visit to her parents was a nightmare as far as Hebe was concerned. How could she possibly manage to convince them that she was marrying Nick because she loved him when every conversation they had seemed to end like this? When it was only on a physical level that the two of them seemed to find any compatibility at all?

'Here.'

She turned to find Nick holding out the ring box from last night.

Her expression darkened as she looked at it. 'I told

you—I don't want it,' she said forcefully. Not even to convince her parents of their relationship could she wear that—that insult of a ring!

Nick sighed heavily. 'Will you just take the damned box, Hebe? So that I can use both hands to drive?' He rasped his impatience with her stubbornness.

She took the box gingerly from his fingers.

'Don't just look at it—open it!' Nick bit out irritably.

She gave him another frowning glance before opening it. Inside was a thin gold band supporting a medium-sized yellow stone surrounded by six smaller diamonds...

'It's a yellow sapphire,' Nick told her abruptly. 'The colour reminded me of your eyes.'

Tears instantly stung those eyes. Something else she had discovered about pregnancy was that tears came all too easily. In fact, emotions altogether came all too easily.

This ring was delicately beautiful—exactly the sort of ring she would have picked herself, given the choice.

And Nick had chosen a yellow sapphire because it matched the colour of her eyes.

'It's beautiful,' she told him breathlessly.

'Then put it on,' he encouraged.

She took the ring from the box and slid it onto the third finger of her left hand. It was a perfect fit.

She looked up at him shyly. 'Did you manage to get your money back on the other one?'

'I didn't even try,' he drawled ruefully. 'I'm keeping it for our tenth wedding anniversary. Or the birth of our fourth child—whichever comes first!'

Fourth child...?

Nick spoke about this marriage as if it would be a permanency rather than an expediency.

Something until this moment Hebe hadn't thought he meant it to be at all.

'It really is a lovely ring, Nick. Thank you,' she told him softly.

'You're actually going to accept this one?' He frowned.

'Of course.' Her voice was huskier than ever.

'Hey, you aren't crying, are you…?' he prompted uncertainly a couple of seconds later, when he obviously heard the sob she had tried so hard to suppress.

She *was* crying. The threatening tears had finally cascaded hotly down her cheeks. They were impossible to control, it seemed.

Nick was going to think she was an idiot, an emotional fool—crying over a ring.

But it wasn't just about the ring.

It was everything. The enormity of her pregnancy. Nick's insistence that she marry him. The uncertainty of what their future together might bring.

Apart from the four children Nick seemed to have planned!

Nick took another hard glance at her before pulling the car over to the side of the country road they were travelling along, putting it in neutral before turning fully in his seat to look at her. 'I guess we can make it three children if the idea of four scares you this much!' he chided, and he took her in his arms.

His teasing just seemed to make her cry all the harder.

Was he ever going to do or say something that *didn't* reduce this woman to anger or tears? When she was like this, she looked so vulnerable, and all he could think about was protecting her.

He didn't remember Sally being this emotional—not even when she had been expecting Luke…

'You aren't going to convince your parents of anything except that I beat you, if we turn up at their place with you looking all red and blotchy from crying,' he drawled.

He was rewarded by a choked laugh as Hebe raised her face to look at him.

Looking decidedly unred and unblotchy, her face was still beautiful in spite of her tears. Nick felt as if he could drown in those misty golden eyes.

But drowning in her beautiful eyes would do him no damned good at all, he told himself firmly, before releasing her to move back behind the wheel and restart the engine, his expression grimly set as he began the last ten miles or so of their journey.

Keep your eye on the ball, Nick, he taunted himself.

Hebe wasn't marrying him because she loved him. This wasn't a love-match at all. She was expecting his baby, and in return she would want certain things from him. That was it.

Fifteen minutes later, when he met Hebe's parents he learnt exactly why she had been so concerned about their reaction to the two of them.

Henry Johnson was a tall, thin, slightly stooped figure— a retired history professor at Cambridge University, no less—and his wife Jean was the sort of round, homely woman whose husband and child were her whole world, who had made a home for them that was as warm and welcoming as she was herself.

There was no way this couple would ever understand the sort of marriage that he and Hebe were going to have!

'Oh, darling Hebe, how wonderful!' her mother said tearfully when Hebe showed her the engagement ring.

Her father gave her a bear hug. 'You might have

brought Nick home to meet us earlier than this,' he chided, but affectionately rather than in genuine rebuke. 'The owner of the Cavendish Gallery, no less,' he added, slightly dazed.

'My fault, sir,' Nick assured him as the two men shook hands. 'It's all happened so quickly. Hebe just knocked me off my feet the first time I saw her!' Literally, as he remembered it!

Henry nodded, as if he perfectly understood how that could happen to a man where his beautiful daughter was concerned.

They were a little older than Nick had expected—both of them in their sixties, he would guess. That meant Henry and Jean must have been in their late thirties when they'd adopted Hebe. Nick wondered why they had left it so late to decide that was what they were going to do.

The ubiquitous English answer to any occasion, a cup of tea, soon appeared—though Henry was profusely apologetic that they didn't have any champagne to toast the happy couple with.

Nick saw Hebe flinch at the description. So much for his assurances that *he* would behave as if they *were* a happy couple; Hebe looked as if she was about to burst out with the truth at any moment, and damn the consequences...

'Tea is fine, sir,' he assured the older man as he took his cup and saucer. 'Hebe can't drink champagne in her condition anyhow,' he added determinedly. 'Not until after the baby is born, in another seven and a half months or so,' he added for good measure.

Let her try to talk her way out of *that!*

Hebe gave Nick an incredulous look as she saw her parents' stunned reaction to his announcement, but met only glittering challenge in his gaze. His hard, uncompromising gaze.

He was leaving her no way out. That cold blue stare told her so only too clearly. She was his. The baby was his.

She had been wavering, it was true. She had looked at her parents and wondered if perhaps they would understand if she confided her pregnancy to them and asked them to help her. But the relaxed way Nick had made his announcement, the possessiveness in his tone, gave her no opening to do that.

As he had known it wouldn't...

Damn him!

'Mum, Dad.' She turned anxiously to her parents. 'I didn't mean to tell you quite as abruptly as that.' She shot Nick a censorious glance before crossing the room to take her mother's hands in hers. 'But Nick and I *are* expecting a baby, early next year.'

'Which means the wedding is going to be very soon,' Nick put in firmly, though his conversation with Hebe the night before had not got that far. 'My lawyers are working on the paperwork at the moment.'

His *lawyers...!*

Why on earth were his lawyers working on their wedding arrangements? Unless Nick intended making her sign one of those pre-nuptial agreements, or something equally cold and calculated?

Well, she wasn't signing anything like that. Not now. Not ever.

But this wasn't the time to argue that point with him. She was too concerned with calming her parents' shock at the rapidity of everything to have time to worry about Nick and his Machiavellian plans.

'Perhaps a small sherry might be a good idea,' her father said weakly, moving to the cabinet to pour three glasses.

One for himself. One for her mother. And one for Nick.

Who wasn't in shock at all. Instead he looked as if he were enjoying every second of this.

'Well, I suppose it's about time I was a grandmother!' Her mother was the first to recover from the shock, squeezing Hebe's hand supportively.

'You don't intend taking our little girl away to America, do you, Nick?' Her father was more practical.

'No, sir,' he assured him easily. 'Hebe has expressed a wish to live in England, and I'm happy to go along with that. Whatever Hebe wants,' he added, with a challenging raise of his brows across the room at her.

Her father gave him a beaming smile, as if he was quite happy with any man who wanted to want to spoil and look after his 'little girl' in the way Nick seemed to want to.

Except that Hebe knew he didn't.

He wanted the baby she carried. And if he had to concede certain things to the baby's mother to achieve that, then he would do so. On his own terms, of course.

But she couldn't let any of her trepidation show in front of her parents. She knew that she had to make them believe she was as happy with the situation as Nick implied he was.

'We'll want you and Daddy to come up to London for the wedding, of course,' she told her mother warmly. 'In fact, you'll probably be our only guests!' She had no idea what arrangements Nick had discussed with his lawyers, but she very much doubted they would involve a big wedding.

'Not at all, Hebe,' Nick put in smoothly. 'Your flatmate will want to come, of course. And any of your friends you can think of. And I've decided to close the gallery for the day, so that all the staff there can attend too. My own parents will be there, naturally. Along with my younger sister and her family.' He met her gaze confrontationally.

She couldn't believe this. She had expected their wedding to be almost a clandestine affair, with as few people as possible knowing it was taking place, and now Nick had announced he was inviting half of London and all of his close family, as well as her own parents.

'I was keeping it as a surprise, honey,' he murmured indulgently, and as he moved to kiss her lightly on the lips, his arm moving about the slenderness of her waist.

For her parents' sake, of course.

As these elaborate wedding plans probably were too.

'We'll be having a reception at one of the leading hotels,' he told her parents, his arm like a steel band around Hebe as he held her tightly—shackled!—to his side. 'I think it might be better if I were to book you a suite there for a couple of nights too. I'm sure Hebe will want her mother to help her get ready on the day—won't you, honey?' Blue eyes glittered down at her with mocking amusement.

Where was all this coming from? Hebe wondered, feeling dazed.

Of course Nick had been married before, so he was probably more cognizant with wedding arrangements than she was, but even so…!

'We do just have one tiny concern.' Nick turned back to her parents. 'Obviously Hebe has told me that she's adopted. I'm sure she was irresistible as a baby,' he added favourably, as Hebe's father frowned slightly. 'We were just wondering if you had any information on Hebe's real parents?' He looked at them enquiringly. 'Obviously with Hebe expecting a baby the medical history of her birth parents would be real helpful,' he added, with country-boy charm.

Which Hebe, knowing him only too well, didn't fall for at all.

She wasn't sure her parents did either. Glancing at her father, she saw he was still frowning and her mother was looking up at him a little anxiously.

'What sort of thing do you want to know?' her father prompted guardedly.

Nick shrugged. 'As I said, just medical history—stuff like that,' he dismissed easily.

He could feel the sudden tension in the room, and wondered if Hebe had noticed it too.

It was a perfectly legitimate question in the circumstances, surely…?

'Perhaps you know the name of Hebe's birth mother?' he continued lightly. 'Or her father, perhaps.'

'No,' Henry answered slowly. 'I don't believe that was ever mentioned to us.'

Was it just his imagination, Nick wondered, or was the other man's reply just a little ambiguous?

'I told you that Mum and Dad wouldn't know, Nick,' Hebe cut in tensely, at the same time smiling reassuringly at her parents. 'Nick is such a fusspot where this baby is concerned.' She attempted to dismiss him. 'I've assured him that I'm perfectly healthy, and that everything with the baby is going to be just fine, too.'

She hadn't assured him of any such thing. And even if she did, he would want a second opinion. A medical opinion. He had yet to tell her, wanting to avoid having another argument and so cause tension before they met her parents, that he had made that particular appointment for Monday afternoon…

Right now, though, he was far from satisfied with the answers he had received from the Johnsons about Hebe's real parents.

'Sometimes when people adopt children, things like medical histories are discussed, aren't they?' he persisted lightly.

'Sometimes I'm sure that they are.' Henry's reply seemed a little guarded.

'But not in this case?'

'No.' There was definite challenge in the other man's expression now.

The atmosphere had changed from warmly congenial to tensely suspicious.

Why?

What did this couple have to hide?

Because they *were* hiding something. Nick was sure of it.

'Oh, well—I just thought it worth asking. But I'm sure that the doctor will be able to check everything out,' he dismissed, with a lightness he was far from feeling.

'I must tell you about the interesting painting Nick came across a week or so ago.' Hebe cut smoothly into the conversation, obviously changing the subject. 'An Andrew Southern portrait. Have you heard of him?' she prompted her parents lightly.

Nick tensed, having no idea where Hebe was going with this conversation. Surely she didn't want her parents to know about that portrait of her? It wasn't exactly the sort of thing you could bring home to show your family—the raw sensuality of the subject—Hebe—was all too obvious!

'Of course we've heard of him, darling,' Henry confirmed mildly. 'One of his paintings is worth a small fortune, surely?' He addressed this remark to Nick.

'Oh, Nick has a very large fortune—don't you, darling?' Hebe prompted challengingly.

Nick had used her parents shamefully to manipulate her, and now she intended doing the same where he was concerned.

She couldn't be sure that Andrew Southern would respond to her letter and the photograph, and if he didn't she needed more information than Nick had given her to be able to continue her own search for the origins of that portrait. To do that she needed a piece of information Nick hadn't yet revealed.

'Not as large as it once was,' Nick muttered tersely, the warning glitter in his eyes more than meeting her challenge.

Hebe turned unconcernedly back to her parents, knowing Nick was furious with her for bringing up the subject of the portrait. Well she couldn't help that. He had asked the questions he wanted answering, without consulting her or warning her, and now she was going to do the same. Whether he liked it or not.

Because she *knew* that portrait wasn't of her, even if he wouldn't accept that it wasn't.

'It's an unseen portrait the artist painted over twenty years ago,' she confided to her parents. 'Nick is so pleased with it—aren't you, darling?' she prompted, with an insincere sweetness she knew he would recognise as such even if her parents didn't.

'Oh, very,' he confirmed tightly.

'How on earth did you find it?' Hebe's mother smiled with interest.

'Hidden away in a house in the north of England,' Nick answered abruptly, obviously not wanting to pursue this subject at all.

Too bad—because Hebe did!

'Yes. What did you say was the name of the original owner, Nick?' Hebe prompted readily, completely putting him on the spot. The increased glitter in his eyes told her how incensed he was.

Well, so what? she thought. At the moment she was more interested in knowing who had been the original owner of her mother's portrait than she was concerned with Nick obvious displeasure.

'I didn't,' Nick came back stiffly, wondering why Hebe was asking this now. 'And I'm sure Henry and Jean aren't interested in this—'

'On the contrary,' Hebe's father interrupted. 'It all sounds fascinating,' the historian in him prompted inquisitively.

Hebe gave Nick another one of those over-sweet smiles, her smile turning to genuine amusement as she saw how annoyed he was.

But, no matter what he might otherwise wish, he couldn't have things all his own way.

As he seemed used to having!

So far today he had bought her an engagement ring it would have been churlish to refuse, tricked her into what sounded like a full-scale wedding rather than the quiet affair she had been expecting, and questioned her adoptive parents about her real parents.

It was time he told her some of the things *she* wanted to know!

'Not really,' he dismissed easily now. 'The man died, his relatives found and then sold the portrait. End of story.'

'And are you going to put it into one of your galleries?' her mother questioned brightly.

'No!' Nick came back harshly.

Hebe turned to look at him frowningly. If he wasn't going to put the portrait in one of his galleries, then what was he going to do with it…?

'No,' he repeated less violently, seeming to force himself to relax, even while he frowned darkly in Hebe's direction. 'I happen to like this portrait and I intend keeping it for myself.'

'But how wonderful!' her mother came back innocently. 'You'll have to let us see it when we come down to London.'

Much to Nick's discomfort and Hebe's amusement!

She had stood all the abuse from Nick she was going to with regard to that portrait. It wasn't a portrait of her, no matter what Nick believed.

She was slightly surprised at his decision not to show the portrait, after going to all that trouble to purchase it, but perhaps he had decided he didn't want his future wife on public display like that?

Or that it would be yet another thing to torment her with when they were alone!

Yes, that sounded more like the Nick she knew and—

She broke off those thoughts abruptly. What was the point of thinking about her love for Nick when she was obviously just another possession to him? A *prize* possession, because she carried his child.

Besides, she still didn't have the answers she was looking for!

'What makes this portrait so interesting, though,' she continued cheerfully, 'is that it isn't listed anywhere as one of the artist's works.'

Nick's gaze narrowed searchingly on Hebe's face. How did she know that? Unless she had been checking up on the portrait herself? Which made no sense to him whatsoever. She *knew* Andrew Southern had painted that portrait of her, whether it was listed or not, so why persist in pushing the subject?

'Perhaps it's a forgery?' Jean mused.

'Oh, no, Jean,' Nick answered the older woman assuredly. 'It's most definitely authentic.'

'Kept hidden away in some man's attic for the last twenty-odd years,' Hebe put in teasingly.

She wasn't going to leave this alone, was she? Nick brooded. She obviously still wanted something from him. But what? And more to the point, why?

'Actually, Jacob Gardner kept it in his— Are you okay there, Jean?' He moved forward quickly to catch her cup and saucer as they seemed to leap out of her hand of their own volition.

'Oh, how silly of me.' Jean got up agitatedly to take the cup and saucer away from him. 'I'll take these things out to the kitchen so that there are no more accidents,' she added swiftly, before picking up the laden tray and bustling from the room, her husband following her a few seconds later.

Nick was left not just with a suspicion, but with the certainty that these two elderly people were hiding something…

He just had no idea what.

A searching look at Hebe showed him that she had seen it too, and was just as puzzled. Her baiting of him to get information had somehow backfired on her in a way she hadn't expected…

CHAPTER EIGHT

'YOUR parents are hiding something.'

Hebe gave Nick a frowning glance as he drove them back to London later that evening.

He was right, of course, though she was loath to admit it. Her parents *were* hiding something. Her mother's accident with her cup and saucer after hearing Jacob Gardner's name mentioned had to be indicative of something.

Hebe just had no idea what it was!

Her father had changed the subject once her parents had returned to the sitting room a few minutes later, going back to talking of the forthcoming wedding—a subject guaranteed to put Hebe herself on edge.

'Of course they aren't,' she defended now, having already decided she would talk to her parents in private about this—probably when they came down to London. No concrete plans had been made on that suggestion, though, and wouldn't be until they all knew the date and time of the wedding. 'You're just imagining things, Nick,' she said airily, not wanting him to pursue this particular subject. 'Now, tell me exactly what paperwork it is that your lawyers are working on?' she added scathingly.

She hadn't forgotten that remark, even if he had hoped she had!

'It wouldn't happen to be a pre-nuptial agreement, would it?' she prompted angrily.

Nick raised dark brows. 'Would you sign it if it were?'

'Absolutely not!' she snapped.

'I didn't think so,' he mused.

'They're an insult to everyone involved,' Hebe told him caustically.

'Most of them aren't worth the paper they're written on, either,' he drawled.

'Oh, I have no doubt that any pre-nuptial agreement *your* lawyers prepared would be watertight!' she replied with disgust.

'Probably,' Nick conceded dryly. 'But that isn't what they're doing, and you wouldn't sign it if they were. The paperwork they're dealing with has to do with the fact that I'm an American getting married in England, so this conversation is rather pointless, wouldn't you say?'

Completely, it seemed, and Hebe turned so Nick couldn't see the embarrassment flooding her cheeks. But she felt happier knowing it was only the legal details of their marriage that Nick's lawyers were dealing with, but now she had nothing to distract her thoughts from slipping back to her parents' odd reaction earlier.

That conversation at her parents' house hadn't gone at all as she had expected. She had thought to get Jacob Gardner's name from Nick, but not the response she had from her parents.

'I guess that was probably the intention,' Nick drawled knowingly.

'I have no idea what you're talking about,' she snapped

resentfully. He was far too astute for comfort, this man she was marrying...

'No?' He quirked dark, sceptical brows over questioning blue eyes. 'Your parents obviously know of your involvement with Jacob Gardner, and they would rather I didn't know about it too—is that what all the mystery is about?'

'I have never been involved with a man called Jacob Gardner!' she protested heatedly. 'I had never even heard his name until you mentioned it!'

'Oh, please, Hebe—your parents had,' he said quietly. 'So you must have told them!'

She'd realized her parents knew the name, but she had no idea how.

Neither did she understand how Nick had jumped to the conclusion that she had known Jacob Gardner in that way. A man who Nick himself said had been quite old when he died.

She shook her head. 'I have no idea why you should think I was ever involved with him!'

'It's quite simple—logical, really, if you think about it.' Nick shrugged, his expression grim. 'Andrew Southern painted that portrait. A portrait that was in Jacob Gardner's possession when he died. In the portrait you're wearing an engagement ring. Emeralds and diamonds, as I recall,' he added hardly. 'Which is why you didn't get emeralds and diamonds from me!'

Hebe had noticed the ring, of course. She just hadn't realised that Nick had...

'I'm not asking you for emeralds and diamonds!' she came back tartly.

'Just as well,' Nick rasped dismissively, knowing that

the thought of Hebe wearing any man's ring but his filled him with jealous fury. She was his, damn it. *His!*

But that ring on her finger in the portrait, the fact that Jacob Gardner had owned the portrait, and Hebe's mother's reaction to the man's name—it was enough to convince him that what he had suspected all along was, in fact, true. Hebe had to have been engaged to Jacob Gardner when she'd had an affair with Andrew Southern!

And the thought of her involved with either man was enough to fill him with a blinding rage!

'You were engaged to Jacob Gardner and you had an affair with Andrew Southern. Just admit it, and then get past it,' he rasped furiously, his hands tight on the steering wheel.

'Let me see if I've got this right?' Hebe turned to him, frowning. 'I was engaged to Jacob Gardner—an obviously wealthy man if he could commission an Andrew Southern portrait of me—and then when I met Andrew Southern I changed my allegiance to him—probably because I discovered he was the wealthier of the two men?' she prompted. 'And when my relationship with both men didn't work out I obviously set out to entrap the owner of the Cavendish Galleries instead! Tell me if I've got any of that wrong, Nick?' she prompted with impatient anger.

No, that sounded about right to him!

He was so angry he wanted to hate her, and yet all he could think about was making love to her instead.

'Where are we going?' Hebe prompted frowningly, as she realised they weren't heading in the direction of her flat.

'My apartment.' Nick tersely confirmed her suspicions.

She swallowed hard, not liking his mood at all. It was

too dark and dangerous for her to feel in the least comfortable with him in the privacy of his apartment. This conversation about Andrew Southern and Jacob Gardner had made him seem almost a stranger.

Which, she accepted resignedly, was precisely what he still was!

'Why?' she prompted softly.

Nick shot her a brief, sardonic sideways glance. 'Maybe I just want to be alone with my fiancée for a while?'

Hebe drew in a ragged breath, knowing exactly what that meant; and Nick making love to her in anger was not something she wanted. 'I don't think so, Nick.'

'Why the hell not?' he bit out roughly.

'You don't need me to tell you that,' she said quietly.

He inhaled and exhaled noisily before answering her. 'I'm not going to hurt you, Hebe,' he finally murmured, self-derisively.

Maybe not physically—after all, he had the baby's welfare to think of!—but emotionally this man would rip her to shreds.

But he didn't need to be in the privacy of his apartment to do that. He could do it with just a glance!

'The opposite, in fact,' he added huskily. 'I'm going to make love to you until you cry out for mercy!'

Hebe knew he could do it too, and there was a melting warmth inside her just at the thought of making love with him again. 'I would rather just go straight home, Nick,' she told him determinedly.

His mouth thinned. 'Am I not to get to spend *any* time alone with you today?'

'We're alone now,' she pointed out ruefully. 'We just don't seem to be communicating too well!'

'We communicate better when we're in bed together, I agree!' he rasped.

Which was exactly where Nick wanted to be right now—in bed with Hebe, breathing in her perfume, touching her, caressing her, feeling her response to him as he buried himself deep in the engulfing warmth of her body.

He ached with wanting her!

In fact, he couldn't ever remember wanting any woman as much as he wanted Hebe. All the time. Able to think of nothing but her when they were apart. Just wanting to kiss and caress her when they were together.

It was like a heated madness, one from which he could find no respite even in sleep. Lying awake most of the previous night as he thought only of the time when he would be with Hebe again.

He had fallen in love with her, he had finally admitted that to himself some time around dawn this morning.

Fallen in love with a woman whose motives he still couldn't trust.

Madness.

But it was a madness that he knew he could do nothing about. He loved Hebe. And even if she hadn't been expecting his baby he knew that he would still have had to make her his own—that he couldn't bear the thought of any other man near her, let alone sharing the intimacies that they had together.

Although he was still unsure why, even though Hebe might have wanted to confirm that Jacob Gardner had still owned the portrait when he died, she had done so in front of her parents.

Despite the explanation he had just given for the other men being in Hebe's life, and the fact that she must have talked to her parents about Jacob Gardner, at least in the past, it just didn't add up for her to involve her parents in that way…

Oh, to hell with it! He was giving himself a headache just thinking about it. Obviously Hebe *had* been involved with both men, and that was an end to it.

'Hebe…?' he prompted tersely at her continued silence.

'What do you want me to say?' she came back wearily, her head resting back on her seat.

'I don't want—' He broke off, drawing in a deep, controlling breath. 'Oh, just forget it. I'm not going to beg!' he assured her hardly; he would rather take another cold shower followed by a restless night than do that!

Hebe eyed him frowningly. She didn't understand him at all. How could he still want to make love to her when he believed she had been involved with one man who had been old enough to be her father and another surely old enough to be her grandfather?

But he obviously did. And he just thought she was being difficult by refusing.

She didn't want Nick making love to her when he was angry, as if to prove a point of ownership. Even in her inexperience, she knew that wasn't how two people making love should be.

She sighed. 'We'll be married soon, Nick. Can't you wait until then?'

His jaw clenched tensely. 'Why the hell should I?'

She gasped. 'I'm not just an object for you to pick up and put down when you please, Nick!'

His jaw clenched grimly. 'I have *never* used you as an object, damn it!'

'That's exactly what you're proposing to do now,' she came back heatedly.

His eyes glittered dangerously as he gave her a brief scathing glance. 'I wouldn't touch you now if you begged me to!' he snapped.

'And that isn't going to happen,' she assured him, just as angrily. If Nick's plans worked out—which she was sure they would—the two of them would be married in a few weeks, and then she would be sharing Nick's bed on a permanent basis.

Oh, God…!

'This way,' Nick instructed her abruptly the following evening, as Hebe began to take her things through to his bedroom. Instead, he lead her into the bedroom next to his, also overlooking the river, and put her suitcase down on the bed before turning to look at her.

If anything, she looked in worse shape than he did!

Which was precisely why, on the journey from her apartment, he had actually decided to put her in the bedroom adjoining his, rather than sharing a bedroom with him.

It had been a tough few days for both of them, he had acknowledged last night, after dropping Hebe off at her apartment and returning home alone, to call his parents and then his younger sister to tell them about the wedding. Natalie had been absolutely agog at the speed with which he was contemplating remarrying.

Explaining about the baby—something that had made his mother cry with happiness and his sister exclaim with joy—had helped, of course, but their curiosity about his future bride, the questions he hadn't been able to answer about Hebe, had made him realise that he and Hebe really did need to take a little time, a step back, in order to get to know each other better before they were married.

Out of bed, that was.

Hebe looked surprised at being put into the spare room.

'After what you said yesterday, I decided it would be better for both of us if you had your own room until after the wedding,' he explained quickly as he easily interpreted her questioning look.

Hebe wasn't sure how she felt about it, she didn't seem to be able to think straight at all today. She had slept badly after the strain of their parting last night, with Nick driving away as soon as she had stepped out of the car.

It had been no good telling herself it was what she wanted. Of course it was—but at the same time she longed for the closeness of making love with Nick, knowing they could reach each other on that level if no other.

To add to her misery, she was still totally bewildered as to what to do about her parents.

They had obviously recognised Jacob Gardner's name when Nick had mentioned it, but she couldn't imagine under what circumstances. The more she thought about it, the more puzzled she became.

She knew what conclusion Nick had come to, but as she knew that certainly wasn't the correct one, she was left to try and work out for herself what it was. Not wanting to talk about an obviously sensitive subject in a telephone conversation with her parents, she would have to wait to talk to them when they came to London for the wedding.

But that hadn't stopped her thinking. And wondering.

Jacob Gardner had lived in the north of England, and to her knowledge her parents had never lived anywhere but Cambridgeshire, their lives completely wrapped up in the university there.

Her parents had never, in the twenty-six years Hebe had been alive, mentioned knowing or befriending a man called Jacob Gardner.

Yet their reaction was undeniable. They had heard the man's name before, if nothing else.

How?

And if they *had* known him why hadn't they exclaimed over the coincidence, rather than behaving as they had, with her mother dropping her cup and saucer, and her father going very quiet?

Round and round her thoughts had gone the night before. And her highly-charged feelings about Nick hadn't helped her relax, either.

Their relationship, precarious at the best of times, looked like standing even less chance of survival if he was going to continue believing she had been intimately involved with two wealthy men she had actually never even met.

'It's lovely—thank you,' she said now, forcing her attention back to her new home.

And it really was a beautiful bedroom, dominated by yet another four-poster bed, with red and gold coverings and drapes. The furniture looked like Louis IV—very ornate, and very different from the more austere furnishings in Nick's adjoining room.

Had this once been Sally's room?

She wasn't sure she could bear it if it had—

'I didn't buy and open the London gallery until two years ago, Hebe,' Nick drawled, in answer to her unasked question, his gaze quizzically mocking as she gave him a sharp look. 'I'm sure you remember the bathroom from your previous—visits,' he added derisively, as he opened the door that went through to the bathroom, separating the two bedrooms.

Of course she remembered the bathroom. She had showered in it the morning after their first night together. And she had been ill in it six weeks later.

It was a room almost as large as the bedrooms, with a huge glass-doored shower in one corner, a large mirrored vanity and two sinks along the back wall, whilst the other wall was taken up by the hugest cream-coloured bath she had ever seen—Jacuzzi bath that looked as if it could seat four comfortably and six rather more—intimately.

'Go ahead and take a bath if you want to,' Nick invited nonchalantly, as he obviously saw her gaze on it and mis-understood the reason for it. 'I have some papers I need to read anyway.'

Consider yourself dismissed, Hebe, she thought with contempt, when she found herself alone in the bathroom a few seconds later.

But it wasn't such a bad idea. She hadn't slept well, and Nick seemed more remote today than he had ever been. She'd also had an emotional parting from Gina an hour or so ago, the two of them having shared the flat for almost a year now, and a nice warm bath would certainly help her to relax.

Wow, she thought admiringly a few minutes later, as she let herself down into the scented, bubbled water, her head resting back against one of the soft waterproof pillows along the edge. Luxury indeed after the cramped bathroom she had shared with Gina. She would fall asleep in here if she wasn't careful!

Hebe looked asleep to Nick as he quietly opened the bathroom door almost an hour later. He hoped she wouldn't think he was intruding on her privacy, but he had been genuinely worried that she had been gone so long—although he had to admit that the thought of Hebe lying naked in the bath had been a constant distraction from his papers...

He might be denied her bed, but that didn't mean he couldn't kiss her, did it?

Hebe felt the nuzzle of lips against her throat first, tensing in surprise, and then relaxing again as she felt the caress of Nick's hands as they travelled down the slope of her breasts to cup and hold them. She felt the instant melting of her body as she looked down to watch the touch of his thumbtips against the pouting nipples.

There was something very erotic about watching those long, tanned, almost disembodied hands as they gently stroked and kneaded her breasts, the fingers first flicking against her sensitised nipples and then squeezing gently, those dual sensations sending a warm melting between her thighs. Her legs parted instinctively, the rhythmic movement of Nick's hands and the added warmth of the water against her sensitivity almost sending her over the edge.

What was Nick doing to her?

One of his hands left her breast to move down the slope of her stomach to the vee between her thighs, unerringly finding the aching nub, caressing her lightly there, all the time with his other hand paying homage to her breast.

Hebe's neck arched and her head fell back as she felt the excitement building inside her, her eyes wide as she found herself looking up into Nick's desire-flushed face.

'Ask me, Hebe,' he prompted fiercely. 'Ask me to keep touching you. *Ask me,* damn it!' he groaned throatily.

At that moment, Hebe knew she would have begged

if Nick had asked her to, so desperately did she feel the need for the touch of his hands and the release only he could give her.

'Please, Nick!' she murmured urgently. 'Please!'

His head swooped down and his lips captured hers fiercely and possessively. He was seemingly pushed beyond the limit of his control. He raised his head to look down at her again, holding her gaze with his as his head moved lower. Hebe's back arched, allowing full access for his lips to capture the breast his hand had forsaken to move between her thighs, and his caress there increase its rhythm as pleasure seemed to rip through every particle of her body.

Hebe collapsed back limply against the side of the bath, satiated beyond belief, beyond possibility.

Nick continued to lick and gently suck the rosy nipple between his lips, enjoying Hebe too much to stop yet, wanting to take her over that edge again and again, until he knew she was utterly, completely his.

She reached her second climax quickly, her whole body shaking with the intensity of her release.

'No more, Nick,' she gasped weakly. 'I can't. Not again!'

'Oh, yes,' he murmured gruffly, sliding into the bath fully clothed. 'You can…!'

And she could, Hebe found, seeing, feeling and knowing nothing but Nick as he took possession of her mouth, his tongue seeking and finding hers, all the time his hands caressing the swell of her breasts and the nipples that were hard and sensitive to the touch.

'I want you, Nick,' she finally gasped, when his mouth released hers to travel down to her breast and draw the tip once more inside, his tongue licking slowly across it. 'I want you inside me. Now!' she murmured achingly, as the pleasure became unbearable, her hips moving rhythmically against his caressing hand.

It was too late. The power of her release this time completely robbed her of breath, a sob of ecstasy catching in her throat.

'I need you inside me, Nick,' she urged, when she finally found breath again to speak. 'Please!' The heated ache inside her cried out for his full possession.

God, she looked wonderful like this, Nick acknowledged heatedly as he stood up with her in his arms and carried her through to the bedroom. He just wanted to make love to her all day long. All week long! Damn it, he never wanted to stop!

But Hebe had her own ideas about that, he quickly learnt. She was kneeling up on the bed to slowly divest him of his wet clothes, her lips leaving a trail of fire over his chilled skin as she slipped the wet shirt from his shoulders, kissing across his shoulders and down his chest, looking up at him with smouldering gold-coloured eyes as she ran her tongue across his own hardened nipple before moving lower to dip erotically into his navel.

God…!

Nick had never experienced anything like this before. The throb of his thighs was becoming unbearable as he strained against the wet denim.

Wet denim that Hebe peeled quickly from his body, releasing him, her hands caressing him lightly there, like butterfly wings, as she kissed the inside of his thighs, her mouth hot and moist. A groan low in Nick's throat escaped as he ached for those lips about him.

'What do you want, Nick?' Hebe prompted huskily as she continued to kiss him, her tongue trailing the length of him now, driving him quietly, madly insane. 'Tell me what you want?'

'For God's sake…' he gasped achingly.

'Tell me, Nick,' she urged softly.

'Take me, Hebe,' he groaned. 'For God's sake—ah…!' Barely had her lips touched him when he realised he had almost reached the point of his own release, knew he was going over the edge, too aroused to stop himself. 'What—?' he cried, as she released him to move above and over him.

Hebe moved slowly, holding Nick's heated gaze as she gradually took the pulsing length of him inside her, breasts thrust forward for his mouth to reach as she began to move above him. His lips found and took one rosy nipple deep inside his mouth as he moved in the same rhythm beneath her.

They reached their climax together, hot, pulsing and explosive, looking into each other's eyes as Hebe arched ecstatically above him before collapsing weakly on his chest.

Amazing.

Incredible.

Unbelievable.

Making love with Nick had to be the most erotic experience of her life!

Nick's arms were wrapped around Hebe, and the silver-gold of her hair draped across his chest as he held her against him, their breathing steadying, the fierce beat of his heart slowly returning to normal.

But deep inside him Nick knew his life would never be normal again.

He had been married for five years, had known women before and since his marriage, but never before had he ever been with anyone like Hebe.

She was magnificent.

An enchantress.

He had thought to possess and bind her to him with the force of their lovemaking, and instead he found himself possessed and bound to Hebe.

For ever.

His arms tightened about her as he dismissed, expelled, any thought that he might ever lose her. That would never happen. He wanted Hebe. And no matter what her reasons for marrying him, he vowed she would stay with him always.

He could no longer contemplate a life without her!

'So much for waiting until after we're married,' she murmured self-derisively.

'You said you wanted me. And I can't keep my hands off you,' he admitted gruffly. 'Not that I tried too hard,' he acknowledged. 'Hebe— Damn!' he muttered impatiently as the telephone on the bedside table began to ring.

Hebe raised her head to look at him, deeply resentful of this interruption to their closeness. 'Leave it, Nick,' she encouraged throatily.

The longer they stayed here, in their own world, without outside influences, the more she hoped that they would come to know and understand each other. They had to if their marriage was to stand any chance at all.

And physically, she knew, they were perfectly attuned. It was a start.

The telephone kept ringing, and by the tenth ring Hebe could see that Nick was becoming restless.

She moved off his chest, smiling slightly. 'Go ahead and answer it,' She nodded. 'It must be something important to keep ringing like that.'

His expression darkened. 'If it isn't, I'm going to wring someone's neck!'

'As long as it isn't mine,' she teased.

He kissed her lingeringly on the lips to dispel that idea, before turning to pick up the receiver. 'Yes? What—?' He sat up in bed, his expression suddenly strained. 'Could you just hold on a minute?' he asked the caller gruffly, even as he swung his legs off the bed. 'I'll put the call on hold and take it in the other room,' he told Hebe abruptly.

Hebe watched him go with languid eyes, admiring the hard nakedness of his body as he strolled across the bedroom, feeling too lazy, too satiated to move.

When Nick came back they would talk. Or rather *she* would talk and Nick would listen. And this time he would believe her. He *had* to!

When Nick came back...

Ten minutes later he still hadn't returned to the bedroom, and the bedcovers were feeling slightly damp and uncomfortable beneath Hebe. She smiled as she realised they had been so desperate for each other that they had lain on the bed together still dripping wet from the bath.

Hebe smiled again dreamily as she got up to go in search of dry bedsheets. There had to be some in the apartment somewhere. And if they were to sleep in that bed tonight the covers would have to be changed first. It—

'That's wonderful, Sally,' she heard Nick murmur huskily in the sitting-room, and came to an abrupt halt as she realised the call had to be from his ex-wife.

A call Nick had deliberately chosen not to take in front of Hebe...

But why would his ex-wife, a woman he had been divorced from for two years, be calling him?

'Yes, of course I'll come and see you when I get back to New York.' Nick spoke gruffly. 'I agree, it's been too long. It's past time we put the past behind us and talked. I'm so glad to give it another try. And, Sally...' Nick paused slightly. 'I can't tell you how pleased I am that you called me like this,' he added warmly.

Hebe beat a hasty retreat—not back to Nick's bedroom, but to her own, tears blurring her vision as she shut the door firmly behind her.

So much for their lovemaking...!

From the brief part of the conversation Hebe had overheard, Sally obviously wanted the two of them to meet and talk about a reconciliation. At least! And it was a sentiment Nick obviously echoed.

What did that make of their own impending marriage? And the baby she carried?

CHAPTER NINE

SHE was no nearer answering those questions the next morning, as she and Nick sat silently at the breakfast bar, neither of them eating, but both having drunk copious cups of coffee since they'd got up just after seven o'clock.

Hebe had been lying in bed pretending she was asleep by the time Nick got off the phone the previous evening, forcing herself not to move or change the even tenor of her breathing as he came into the room and looked down at her, calling her name softly, sounding puzzled rather than annoyed when she didn't respond.

She hadn't been asleep, of course. How could she possibly have slept when she had no idea what was going to happen next?

Surely the fact that Sally had telephoned Nick now, when he was on the eve of marrying someone else, had to be significant?

If nothing else, it was a case of dog-in-a-manger: Sally couldn't live with Nick herself, but she didn't want anyone else to have him either!

And, if that were true, the other question was how had Sally known Nick was going to remarry? Logically it had to be either Nick himself who had told her—although that was unlikely, in view of his initial surprise at Sally's call. It must have been a member of Nick's family who had chosen to impart that information to his first wife.

Anyway, it didn't matter how the other woman had found out. Her motive for calling Nick had been obvious and the closeness Hebe and Nick had shared had been totally shattered by her call.

In fact, Hebe had ended up crying herself to sleep. She was angry with Nick. But she was angry with herself too! Angry because a part of her had still wanted to get up out of her bed and go to him, to lose herself in his arms once again.

She stood up abruptly. 'I had better be getting to work—'

'Don't be silly, Hebe.' Nick turned to her impatiently. He looked as if he hadn't slept too well the previous night, either, and his temper was on a very short fuse. 'I spoke to Jane and told her you won't be working at the gallery any more.'

Hebe eyes flashed deeply gold. 'Then you had better just go and tell her differently, hadn't you?'

Nick scowled. 'And why would I do that?'

'Because until Gina finds someone else to share the flat with her I intend paying my half of the rent, and I need a job to be able to do that. Besides,' she added irritably, '*I'll* decide when and if I leave my job!'

Nick eyed her impatiently. 'Not if I decide to sack you first,' he bit out tersely.

'You can try,' Hebe challenged. 'That should look quite interesting in the newspapers—Wife Sues Husband for Unfair Dismissal!'

Nick drew in a long, controlling breath in an effort to hold on to his already tightly stretched temper. 'Hebe, as my wife you will have no need to work. Ever again.'

Angry colour flared in the pallor of her cheeks. 'I'm not your wife yet—'

'Semantics—'

'Sense,' she came back forcefully. 'I do have rent to pay.'

'I'll pay your damned rent until Gina finds someone else,' he snarled, impatient with her stubbornness.

Just impatient, really. He hadn't been able to believe it when he'd got back to his bedroom last night and found Hebe gone.

She hadn't been in the bathroom or the kitchen when he'd looked, leaving only the spare room. And that was where he'd found her, curled up in the bed there, fast asleep!

She hadn't responded to the soft prompting of calling her name, either, and other than actually shaking her awake Nick had had no choice but to leave her there and go back to his own bedroom.

To a soaking wet bed!

By the time he had completely changed the bedclothes and got into bed himself he had been wide awake, staring at the portrait he had brought up from his office the previous day.

Hebe…

He could just see himself in the years to come, Nick brooded, staring at a portrait of the woman he loved because the reality still eluded him. Just like Jacob Gardner, damn it!

Another night without sleep certainly hadn't calmed his annoyance.

As Hebe was learning only too well!

She stiffened resentfully at his dictatorial tone. 'I don't need you to pay my rent or anything else! If something should go wrong with this pregnancy—'

'What do you mean, go wrong?' Nick pounced harshly, his frown fierce.

'No, Nick—I wouldn't do anything to harm this baby,' she sighed wearily as she saw the accusation in his eyes. 'According to your theory of my being a gold-digger that wouldn't serve my purpose at all, now, would it?' She gave a derisive shake of her head. 'But if anything should go wrong you won't want me as your wife any more, will you? Which means I'll need a job!' she scorned.

Though she somehow couldn't see herself continuing to work for Nick—or him letting her do so—if the two of them divorced.

Nick glowered at her for several long seconds. 'That won't happen,' he finally growled. 'And if it should I'll just get you pregnant again!'

Her eyes widened. 'Why on earth would you want to repeat the same mistake with a little gold-digger like me?'

His mouth twisted scornfully. 'For exactly that reason,' he told her coldly. 'There is no way I am ever going to let you divorce me, Hebe!'

Hebe realized that was because Nick believed a divorce would result in a divorce settlement—the handing over to her of lots of Cavendish money—and he had no intention of that ever happening!

'Fine,' she snapped. 'But even as your wife I'll decide what I'm going to do, not you!'

He closed his lids briefly, his eyes deeply blue when he opened them to look at her once again. 'You're just spoiling for a fight this morning, aren't you?'

She stiffened. 'Not that I'm aware of, no.'

'Liar,' he muttered disgustedly, his gaze probing now.

'And I'm not exactly in a good mood myself,' he warned her unnecessarily. 'Why the hell had you disappeared when I came back to bed last night?'

Hebe avoided that searching gaze, not wanting him to so much as guess that she had overheard some of his conversation with his ex-wife. That would be just too embarrassing. Besides, with the opinion Nick already had of her as a schemer, he would probably think she had listened to his telephone call on purpose.

She shrugged dismissively. 'I was tired, so I went to bed.'

Nick breathed deeply through his nose as he continued to look at her. 'You were already *in* bed—'

'But not my own bed,' she insisted.

He shook his head frustratedly. 'You don't seriously think I'm going to let you continue to sleep in another room after last night?'

'That's exactly what I think,' she dismissed, turning away, wondering when—or if—he was ever going to tell her that it had been Sally who'd telephoned him yesterday evening.

Probably never, she decided heavily.

After all, he had loved Sally, and their child had been born into a marriage of love. This child would be born into a marriage of convenience. If their marriage still went ahead, that was.

'As I said, I'm going to work now,' she told him stiffly.

Going down two floors to work was going to be convenient, at least. It was about the only convenience for her that she could think of in connection with this marriage.

'Only until lunchtime,' Nick informed her flatly. 'You have an appointment with an obstetrician at two o'clock this afternoon,' he explained at her questioning look.

Hebe's eyes widened as she turned back to look at him.
'I thought I told you—'

'Hebe, in view of your negative comments, I had the
other guy's secretary recommend another obstetrician.' He
scorned her objection.

'You did?' She eyed him uncertainly.

His mouth twisted ruefully. 'I did.'

'I bet you were popular!' she mused.

Nick shrugged. 'I'm not out to win any popularity
contests—as I'm sure you know only too well!' he added
hardly.

Hebe's humour instantly disappeared. What was she
smiling about when she was still so angry and upset with
him over that telephone call from Sally last night? She
was so confused by her own feelings for him, that she
could cheerfully have hit him over the head with his own
coffee mug!

'Oh, yes,' she agreed derisively. 'I'm well aware of that!'

'Good.' Nick stood up abruptly. 'I'm going down to my
office this morning, to deal with paperwork. We'll meet up
here for lunch at about twelve-thirty—'

'You're expecting me to start cooking for you already?'

His eyes glittered deeply blue. 'I usually have a
sandwich for lunch. Which I'm quite capable of getting for
myself. And you too, if necessary. I intend making sure that
you eat properly in future,' he added.

'Like a brood mare!' she flung back scathingly.

Nick took a step towards her, his face dark with fury
now, hands tightly clenched at his sides.

Totally intimidating, Hebe acknowledged warily.

Nick's eyes narrowed as he sensed her apprehension,
and he forced himself to relax, his expression noncommit-

tal, hands loose at his sides. 'I think it might be better if you don't bait me like that again, Hebe,' he warned softly.

Her chin rose defiantly. 'And if I do?'

Nick gave a humourless smile. 'Then you're going to get just what you're asking for!'

She swallowed hard, and moistened her kissable lips with the tip of her tongue.

Instantly shooting Nick's temperature sky-high and creating an ache in his body.

He could visualise only too easily where those lips and tongue had been last night, and he burned to make love to her again.

She raised dark blonde brows. 'And what's that?'

He forced a mocking smile, inwardly fighting his need to take her in his arms and forget everything but the two of them. Which, from their uncontrollable response to each other, he knew he could do. It was only that Hebe was likely to hate him for it. Hate him more, that was…

'Exactly the same as you got last night,' he drawled in answer to her challenge. 'Probably with a few variations—I wouldn't want you to get bored with sharing my bed!'

Her eyes widened. 'You're blaming *me* for last night?'

He shook his head, his smile humourless. 'I don't think you can attach blame to something so mutually satisfying—do you?'

Hebe's cheeks felt fiery red, and she was unable to deny her response to him. Her only consolation was that Nick seemed to want her as much as she wanted him.

'I'm going to work,' she repeated abruptly.

'We'll make a move from here at about one-thirty—'

'*We'll* make a move?' she echoed, turning slowly.

Nick eyed her scornfully. After losing Luke, there was

no way he was going to miss out on any part of his new baby's life. 'You don't seriously think I'm going to let you go to the doctor's alone, do you?'

She simply hadn't given it any thought at all. She wasn't used to being a couple, to having someone else around all the time.

And after Nick's obvious warmth to Sally on the telephone last night, and the fact that the two of them were obviously going to see each other the next time Nick was in New York, it might be as well if she didn't get used to it, either!

'I'm not a child, Nick,' she snapped. 'I am capable of getting myself wherever I want to go!'

'But why take the tube or a cab when I'm offering to drive you? Besides,' he added grimly, 'I want to hear what the doctor has to say.'

Hebe tensed. 'Why?'

'Because it's my baby too!' he came back with controlled force. 'And the sooner you get used to that idea, the easier things are going to be!'

Yes, it *was* Nick's baby too, she accepted heavily. No matter what the reason for Sally Cavendish's call the previous evening, or whether she and Nick became reconciled emotionally Hebe knew that Nick took the responsibility of his child seriously. It was the only reason she was here in his life at all...

And she mustn't ever lose sight of that fact.

As she almost had last night.

She just had no defences, no way of resisting, when Nick touched her. And it was no good pretending that she did.

Nick watched their motions flickering across her expressive face—the uncertainty, the apprehension.

Damn it, he didn't want this woman to be frightened

of him! He wanted the impossible— this marriage somehow to work, for the two of them to reach some sort of understanding.

Quite how he went about achieving that, when all they did when they weren't in bed together was argue, he had no idea.

Maybe if they tried to stop arguing it might be a start...

'Look, Hebe, let's call a truce, shall we?' he prompted gently. 'This constant bickering isn't doing a damn thing for me, and I doubt it is for you either.'

She eyed him mockingly. 'Don't try and pretend it's *me* you're concerned about, Nick—'

'Will you just stop?' he ground out frustratedly, grasping her shoulders to shake her slightly, her hair a silken tumble about her shoulders. 'I don't want to argue with you any more—okay?'

She grimaced, golden eyes troubled. 'Your moods are so unpredictable...'

He gave a hard laugh. 'Is there anywhere that says an expectant father has to be predictable?'

'I suppose not,' Hebe allowed with a sigh. 'But I might be able to understand you better if you were.'

Nick raised dark brows, his gaze searching on the pale beauty of her face. 'Do you *want* to understand me?'

A shutter seemed to come down over those expressive eyes, her expression once more defensive. 'Not particularly,' she dismissed scathingly.

Well, *he* wanted to understand her!

Last night, with Hebe, had been the closest thing to perfection he had ever known in his life. No, it hadn't been just close—it had been perfection.

He refused to believe Hebe could have been with him

like that, given of herself like that, without feeling something more for him than appreciation for his millions!

Unless he was just deluding himself…?

He released her abruptly, turning away. 'You're right.
It's past time we were both getting to work.'

'Yes, sir!' Hebe came back tauntingly.

Nick closed his eyes briefly before walking away. He
had to walk away, otherwise he really might do something
he would regret.

Hebe watched Nick leave, her heart heavy, knowing
that the closeness they had reached last night before Sally's
call really had been a myth—that they had no common
ground but the baby she carried.

The next seven and a half months, until her body became
her own once more, loomed over her like a dark shadow.

Work—that was the answer. She had always loved her
job at the gallery, and even knowing of Nick's brooding
presence up in his office on the second floor wouldn't rob
her of that pleasure today. She quickly lost herself in her
work once she had explained to Jane, the manager, that
Nick had been mistaken, and she intended working for
several more months yet.

Her colleagues were agog with curiosity, of course, and
eyed her ring enviously, which made things a little
awkward. But once they realised Hebe was just her normal
self, even if she was shortly going to marry the owner of
the gallery, they all settled down to the easy friendship they
had always enjoyed.

Well, more or less, Hebe acknowledged ruefully.

There were no more comments in her hearing about
their gorgeous boss, or any wondering about what Nick
looked like naked, but if that was the only change in their

behaviour, Hebe could certainly cope with that. In fact, talking about Nick like that wasn't something she wanted to do right now, anyway!

It was her hormones that caused this weakness in her legs and the ache in her body whenever she thought of him, she tried to convince herself. They were all haywire because she was expecting a baby, that was all.

She repeated that to herself when Nick walked into the gallery later that morning, and she felt the heat course through her body just looking at him.

He really was as gorgeous as her work colleagues said he was—and she had very good reason to know exactly how Nick looked naked!

She tensed as he strode forcefully down the gallery towards her with his usual vitality, remembering how she had run her fingers through that overlong dark hair last night, how muscled that body was beneath the tailored grey suit he wore.

'Yes?' She faced him defensively.

'We have an audience, Hebe,' Nick murmured softly with a pointed look at Kate, working further down the cavernous gallery. 'Is that all the greeting you have for your fiancé?'

She shot him an irritated glance. 'So you want us to maintain a certain—discretion in front of the rest of your employees, don't you?'

No, not really, he thought. Discretion was the last thing that came to mind in connection with his thoughts about Hebe! And she wasn't just an employee, for God's sake, she was his fiancée.

'I thought that would be what you'd want,' he drawled dryly. 'I also thought you might like to know that my lawyers have telephoned, and the wedding has been arranged—two weeks on Friday, two-thirty in the afternoon,' he informed her with satisfaction—and watched as her face paled in response to the news that she was marrying him in eighteen days' time.

Damn it, why did she always act as if marrying him was almost as bad as being marched to the gallows, instead of a wedding to a man who had more money than she could spend in a lifetime?

'I thought you might like to call your parents and let them know now that we have a definite date and time,' he rasped.

'I tried calling them earlier, but there was no answer,' she revealed with a slight frown.

Nick tensed, wondering why, when she had only seen them on Saturday, she should have tried to call them this morning. 'Oh?'

Hebe grimaced. 'They're usually at home on a Monday morning.'

He shrugged. 'Perhaps this Monday morning they decided to do something different.'

'Maybe.' She nodded, obviously not satisfied.

Nick frowned. 'I'm sure it's nothing to worry about, Hebe.'

She had tried *not* to, but the more she had thought about it the more convinced she had become that her parents had behaved very strangely on Saturday after Jacob Gardner's name had been mentioned. Her call to them this morning had been an effort to reassure herself that they hadn't— only to have the phone ringing and ringing their end, remaining unanswered.

'I'll call them back later,' she dismissed now, not wanting Nick to realise how troubled she was.

'Maybe—'

'Nick—Hebe. I'm sorry to interrupt.' A slightly breathless Jane approached them. 'But you have visitors.'

'Just put them in a room somewhere and I'll be out shortly,' Nick said, with obvious impatience.

'Actually, it's Hebe who has visitors,' Jane corrected awkwardly.

'I do…?' Hebe's eyes widened in surprise.

Jane nodded. 'They say they're your parents—'

Hebe didn't wait for the other woman to finish, and turned sharply on her heel to hurry from the room, not knowing whether Nick followed her or not—although she thought he probably would.

She had no idea what her parents were doing here, of all places, but at least she now had an answer as to where they had been this morning…!

CHAPTER TEN

NICK'S long strides easily caught up with Hebe's shorter ones as she left the gallery, and he was at her side when they reached the huge marble entrance hall where Jean and Henry stood waiting.

He felt glad that he was there when he saw the strain on the older couple's faces, more sure than ever that the disquiet he had felt on Saturday had been justified.

'I hope you don't mind, Nick?' Jean said anxiously, even as she clasped both Hebe's hands in hers. 'We need to talk to Hebe. To both of you,' she added softly.

'If we could go somewhere—less public?' Henry prompted quietly, as half a dozen people passed them on their way into the gallery.

'Mum? Dad?' Hebe frowned her concern as she looked at them both. 'What's wrong? Has something happened?'

'We just need to talk to you, darling.' Her mother squeezed her hands reassuringly. 'We—have some things to explain.' She looked pained at the admission.

'We'll go upstairs to my apartment,' Nick decided briskly. 'Hebe?' he prompted pointedly, as she made no effort to move, her face pale as she looked searchingly at her mother.

Jean, he could easily see, was under extreme emotional pressure. Her eyes looked red and tearful; her face was as white as Hebe's.

Whatever was going on here, Nick intended being at Hebe's side when it happened. Whatever it was!

Hebe could feel her tension rising with the lift as it ascended, wondering if what her parents needed to talk to her so urgently about had something to do with Jacob Gardner.

She knew that Andrew Southern must have received her letter and photograph by now, and that even though she had given him the address of her flat, and the number of her mobile if he should want to contact her, there had been no response from him.

She was disappointed—deeply so. But if her parents could tell her something about Jacob Gardner that would at least be something.

Although she wasn't at all happy at the stress her parents appeared to be under...

'Here we go.' Nick led the way into his apartment.

Their apartment now, Hebe supposed, wondering if her parents had tried to contact her at her old flat before coming here, and been surprised when Gina told them she had moved out. She had thought to save that little piece of information until her parents came to London for the wedding, deciding there was no point in their knowing before then.

Little had she known they were going to surprise her with a visit.

'You look as if you could do with something to drink, Jean?' Nick frowned. 'Henry?'

'Perhaps a small glass of brandy,' her father accepted gruffly.

To Hebe's knowledge her father only ever drank brandy when he was sick or worried about something; looking at him, at both her parents, it was easy to see that this time it was the latter.

'What's wrong?' she prompted again, once the drinks had been poured and they were all seated in the sitting room.

Her mother gave a shaky sigh. 'We should have told you at the weekend,' she said, flustered. 'Your father wanted to tell you then.' She gave him a rueful smile. 'But I begged him not to. I see now that he was right all along—that we should have told you years ago.' She shook her head sadly.

'Told me what?' Hebe pressed anxiously, her tension increasing by the second.

Nick moved to stand behind Hebe's chair, quietly supportive—whether she wanted his support or not.

Which she probably didn't, he accepted heavily—but she was going to get it anyway!

'About your mother,' Henry said, taking charge of the conversation.

'My—mother…?' Hebe repeated slowly.

Hebe's mother? Nick repeated too, inwardly, having been sure that this conversation was going to be about Jacob Gardner after Jean's reaction to his name at the weekend.

What did Hebe's *mother* have to do with Jacob Gardner?

Besides which, hadn't Jean and Henry assured him on Saturday that they had no knowledge of Hebe's mother?

No…he suddenly realised. What Henry had actually said was that the name of Hebe's father had never been mentioned…

Nick had thought the other man's reply ambiguous at the time. Now he realised why!

'What do you know about Hebe's mother?' he prompted harshly.

'Please, Nick.' Hebe turned to him pleadingly. 'Let them—let them tell this in their own time.'

She had a feeling she knew at least part of what her parents were going to say, as she was sure now that they had known of her mother's connection to Jacob Gardner all along—if not to Andrew Southern. They probably knew her name too.

Hebe had no idea why they would have kept such a thing from her, as they had always been so open about everything else, and had brought her up to be the same way. They must have had a good reason for not telling her about her mother. And, having seen the portrait, with its overt sensuality, she could perhaps guess what that reason was.

'You asked about the medical history of Hebe's real parents on Saturday, Nick,' her father reminded the younger man ruefully. 'I told you then that we had no idea. I wasn't exactly truthful. We really don't know anything about Hebe's real father.' His voice hardened slightly. 'But now we know of Hebe's pregnancy, we—'

'Your mother died in childbirth, Hebe,' her mother told her emotionally. 'She was so tiny, so delicate, and they left it too late to do anything about it. The birth went terribly wrong, and—and she died and the baby lived. *You* lived.' Tears glistened, and then fell from pained brown eyes.

It was all too much for Hebe to take in. Her mother was *dead*.

It was a possibility she had never even thought of.

When she had first learnt of her adoption, before dismissing the whole thing as unimportant, she had imagined lots of reasons why her mother had given her up. Perhaps she had been very young, a single mother, or even a married woman who hadn't been able to support another child in the family. But death—death had never been an option...

The woman in the portrait, so young and alive, had *died* giving birth to her?

It didn't seem possible. It was a cruelty that shouldn't have been allowed.

Like the death of Nick's son Luke...

She turned to him as his hand came down firmly on her shoulder. 'I can't—' She shook her head. 'I can't believe it, Nick—can you?'

Oh, he could believe it, all right. It wasn't the believing of it that was the problem!

He fixed his glittering gaze on her parents. 'Are you saying—are you telling us that Hebe may have a similar medical problem when she gives birth to our baby?' He had caught the relevance of Jean's statement even if Hebe hadn't.

'It's a possibility.' Henry was the one to answer him. 'Can you see why we had to tell you?'

'I can see why you should have told us on Saturday, not waited until now—'

'Nick!' Hebe cautioned emotionally.

He shook his head impatiently. 'I'm sorry, Hebe, but your parents knew all the time that your mother had died in childbirth, knew the risk of the same thing happening to you, and yet only now—' He broke off abruptly, turning sharply to look searchingly at the older couple.

There was something else significant in what Jean had just said about Hebe's mother...

'How do you *know* that Hebe's mother was, to quote you, Jean, "so tiny, so delicate"?' he prompted shrewdly.

'You're an intelligent man, Nick,' Henry complimented

him gruffly. 'The reason we know those things is because Claudia, Hebe's mother, was our daughter.'

It was Nick's turn to be left speechless.

And if *he* was stunned by this revelation, how much more shocked must Hebe feel?

Except she didn't appear shocked when he glanced down at her. Instead there was an excited glow in her golden eyes as she turned to him, a look of anticipation on her face.

'Would you go and get the portrait, Nick?' The animation was audible in her voice.

'Portrait?' He frowned his confusion.

'*The* portrait, Nick,' she said, very firmly.

What the hell did she want her portrait for now? Why show *that* to her adoptive parents—her grandparents?—at all? They were talking about her mother, for God's sake—

Nick froze. 'Hebe…?' he questioned slowly.

She nodded. 'Please.'

Nick moved to his bedroom as if in a dream, a truth—a startling truth—hitting him right between the eyes.

A truth he had scorned.

A truth he had accused Hebe of lying about.

The woman in the portrait *was* her mother!

'Are you okay, darling?' Hebe's mother prompted anxiously once they were alone. 'We shouldn't have deceived you, I know…'

'I'm okay,' Hebe assured her warmly. 'I'm not too sure about Nick, though,' she added ruefully, having seen the stunned look on his arrogantly handsome face as he went into his bedroom.

'You're not upset or angry, or feeling we've let you down, because all this time we've never told you we're your grandparents and not your adoptive parents?' her mother probed emotionally.

It was a little strange, Hebe had to admit, but at the same time it all made perfect sense. Her mother—Claudia—had died giving birth to her, and so Claudia's parents had taken Hebe in as their own.

She stood up, moving to hug the people who had been the only parents she knew. Kind, giving people, who had loved her and cared for her all her life. How could she possibly be angry with them? Whatever they had done, she was sure they had done it out of love and nothing else.

She smiled tearfully as she stood back. 'How could I possibly be angry with you? You did what you thought was best, I'm sure.'

'We still should have told you,' her father admitted heavily. 'But we had lost Claudia, and you—you were so like she was as a baby.' His voice grew husky with emotion. 'A tiny little thing, with a mop of blonde hair. We loved you on sight. And we had made so many mistakes with Claudia, it seemed. We so wanted a second chance with you.'

'A second chance…?' Hebe had time to ask curiously, before Nick came back into the room with the portrait.

She crossed the room to his side. 'Just stand it on the sofa, would you, please, Nick?' she requested softly, knowing by the grim expression on his face that he was still far from satisfied with the explanation they had been given.

Well, maybe once her parents had seen Claudia's portrait he would be given an explanation he could accept!

Nick heard Jean give a pained gasp as he stood the portrait up against the back of the sofa, turning to see Henry walking dazedly across the room for a closer look, the lines of strain on his face making him look every one of his sixty-odd years.

Henry reached out a hand, just as Hebe had the first time she'd seen the portrait, not quite touching the canvas, but almost tracing a hand lovingly over the creamy contours of the beautiful face.

'Tell me, Dad,' Hebe said softly as she stood beside him in front of the portrait. 'Did Claudia have a birthmark?'

'She did.' Jean was the one to answer as she moved to join her husband and granddaughter. 'A tiny red rose-shape, just—there…!' She gasped as she saw the portrait fully. 'Claudia…!' she cried brokenly, her tears falling in earnest now as she gazed in awe at the portrait. 'But how…?'

'It's the portrait I told you about on Saturday—the one that Nick found hidden away in a man's house after he died,' Hebe explained happily.

'Jacob Gardner's house,' Nick put in harshly, wishing he felt as happy as she did about all of this.

This portrait obviously *was* of Claudia Johnson, as Hebe had always claimed it was. Henry and Jean's reactions to seeing it were too genuine for it to be otherwise. But if that was true then it made a complete nonsense of the things Nick had accused Hebe of doing. Accusations she had vehemently denied. He had called her a liar. A liar and a gold-digger…!

Henry turned to look at him questioningly. '*This* is the Andrew Southern portrait you told us about?'

'Yes,' Nick bit out tautly.

'Twenty-seven years ago, Claudia was engaged to a man called Jacob Gardner.' Jean sighed. 'He was much older than her, thirty years or so, but he was very wealthy, and when he asked her to marry him she accepted.'

'And then she met Andrew Southern and fell in love with him instead,' Nick grated grimly.

Everything he had accused Hebe of doing, in fact.

Accused and punished her for. His jealousy of the other men such that he had wanted to make Hebe his over and over again, in order to banish them from her mind and heart.

Dear God, how she must hate him!

He couldn't even look at her at this moment. He needed time in which to re-evaluate this whole situation.

And time, it seemed, was something he didn't have.

'We don't know that for certain,' Hebe spoke quietly. 'Although admittedly this portrait looks as if it was painted by a man who—*knew* his subject more intimately than an artist and his model.'

She couldn't quite look at her parents. Claudia might have been her biological mother, but she was a woman Hebe had never known. Whereas she had been Henry and Jean's daughter—someone Jean had given birth to, that the two of them had brought up and loved.

'We don't really know what their relationship was,' she added firmly.

'I can't believe this is our Claudia.' Her mother still gazed tearfully down at the portrait. 'She was so beautiful, wasn't she? She was absolutely adorable as a child, too. It was only when she got to about sixteen that—well—' She broke off, looking to her husband for assistance.

'She became a little wild.' Hebe's father spoke sadly, shaking his head. 'We don't know where we went wrong. She started going out all the time, sometimes staying out all night. And when we tried to talk to her she just shrugged it off as fussing and carried on exactly the same as before. And then finally—finally she ran away from home, when she was seventeen.' He sat down abruptly in one of the armchairs.

'She had such a love of life,' Jean added chokingly. 'But we didn't know what to do with her any more—couldn't seem to reach her. She ran off, didn't contact us for months, and then it was only the one letter. We didn't even know she was pregnant until we received an urgent telephone call from the hospital. We were too late. When we got there Claudia had already died,' she sobbed. 'But there was Hebe,' she said, smiling through her tears. 'And we believed we had been given a second chance, that with Hebe we would not make the same mistakes.' Tears began to fill her eyes once more.

'You didn't make any mistakes,' Hebe hastened to assure her, holding tightly on to her mother's hand. 'Not with Claudia or with me. You're the best parents anyone could ever have,' she said with certainty. 'And if she had been given the time Claudia would probably have calmed down, settled down, maybe even married and provided you with lots more grandchildren.'

'As it was, it broke our hearts when she ran off like that,' Henry continued heavily. 'Not knowing where she was, what she was doing. Then, as Jean said, after six months of silence she wrote to us, without giving us an address to write back, to say she had a job singing in a hotel in the north of England somewhere—'

'Leeds,' Nick put in quickly.

'Yes, that's right.' Hebe's father nodded. 'She met Jacob Gardner there one evening when he went in to have dinner with friends. Apparently he fell in love with her on sight. She was so excited about her engagement. She wrote that she would bring him down to meet us before the wedding.'

He sighed heavily. 'It all seemed so incredible, so—' He shook his head. 'She was only eighteen years old.'

Hebe looked at the portrait, at her mother, eighteen years old, with all her life ahead of her. Within a year she had been dead.

Nick looked at the portrait too, at those differences Hebe had insisted existed. Apart from the birthmark, the woman in the portrait still looked like a slightly younger version of Hebe to him, if a more knowing, more feral version of her.

But it *wasn't* Hebe.

No wonder she had been so angry with him for not believing her when she'd claimed it wasn't her. When she had denied ever having been engaged to Jacob Gardner or having an affair with Andrew Southern either.

Which meant her innocence completely undermined his other accusation—that she was a gold-digger...

He looked at Hebe now, at those beautiful eyes that entranced him, the sensual fluidity of her body that enraptured him, her intelligence that enthralled him.

And he knew that she didn't want his money at all—that *he* was the one who had assumed that rather than Hebe ever having said that was what she wanted. Now he realised that she had only agreed to marry him because he had threatened her—threatened to take her baby away from her if she didn't.

Thinking of Luke, of his own pain when he'd died, of how Sally's heart had been broken when she'd lost her child, he knew Hebe must hate him for threatening to do the same to her if she didn't marry him.

Had he expected, had he *seriously* expected them to make a marriage based on his threats and Hebe's fear that he might take her baby from her if she didn't stay with him?

The signs had all been there if only he hadn't been blinded by his own unforgiving attitude: the fact that Hebe wouldn't accept that huge diamond engagement ring, her disgust over the expensive car, her refusal to leave her job and be kept by him. But he had chosen to think she was just acting as if she wasn't interested in those things, that the demands would begin once they were married.

What sort of hardened cynic had he become?

More to the point, how could he ever hope to have Hebe fall in love with him after the way he had treated her?

'You don't think that Jacob Gardner was your father?' Jean was the one to prompt Hebe softly.

Hebe gave a rueful smile. 'Look at the portrait, Mum. What do *you* think?'

'Hmm.' Her mother grimaced. 'I think Andrew Southern was in love with Claudia.'

'But was Claudia in love with him? That's the question.' Hebe shrugged.

'I think so,' her father answered consideringly. 'Look at Claudia's face—that glow. It's the glow of a woman who has just been thoroughly loved,' he acknowledged with a wince. 'What do you think, Nick?'

'I think it's not the sort of portrait you would hang over the family fireplace,' Nick acknowledged stiffly.

'Only in a man's bedroom, hmm?' Hebe turned to mock him, only to find herself frowning when she saw the grim expression on his face, felt the restless anger emanating from him.

What was wrong with him?

She had tried to tell him all these things when he'd first showed her the portrait, that it wasn't her but her mother, so why—?

That was what was wrong with him. The fact that she had been right. And he had been wrong. About her, most of all.

Hebe gave him a searching look, and Nick, becoming aware of that look, turned to her with glittering blue eyes so fierce and angry that she only just stopped herself taking a step back from him.

Obviously Nick didn't like to be wrong!

'I also think,' Nick bit out forcefully, 'that with Claudia and Jacob Gardner both dead, there is only one person left in this triangle who can tell us the truth. It's Andrew Southern we need to talk to next.'

'I've already tried to contact him—with no luck,' Hebe revealed with a disappointed shrug.

'You have?' Nick frowned darkly.

'Yes, I have,' she confirmed defensively. 'I gave his agent a letter and a photograph to forward on to him last Friday. No response, I'm afraid,' she confided to her parents.

'A photograph?' Nick prompted suspiciously.

'Of me,' Hebe told him dryly. 'You said it yourself, Nick. My likeness to the woman in the portrait, to Claudia, is too much of a coincidence for it to be accidental. I was hoping that Andrew Southern would think so too, would realise that I have to be Claudia's daughter, and possibly his too. But he hasn't responded, so I guess that theory was wrong.'

And she had been so hopeful too—had hoped to be able to throw the truth in Nick's face once she had it, to prove that the things he believed about her were completely untrue.

Of course Jean and Henry had done that for her by explaining exactly who Claudia was, but she was still disappointed that Andrew Southern hadn't even bothered to so much as acknowledge her letter.

'Not necessarily,' Nick muttered grimly. 'It's only

Monday now, Hebe,' he said. 'We have no idea when his agent forwarded the letter; Andrew Southern may not even have received it yet.'

She supposed that could be a possibility…

'So you think I could still hear from him?' she asked slowly.

'I believe it's a possibility, yes.' Nick nodded tersely. 'And if you don't, I'll go and see his agent myself. You need to get to the bottom of this.'

She did?

Or Nick did?

'In the meantime,' Nick added briskly. 'Hebe has an appointment with a specialist this afternoon; we'll talk to him about Claudia's medical history, and ask him to check whether or not Hebe could have a smiliar problem.'

Hebe had forgotten all about her doctor's appointment this afternoon in the excitement of this conversation.

But Nick obviously hadn't…

He couldn't seriously think that just because her mother had died in childbirth she might too, could he?

Even if he did, hadn't he realised yet that it would solve all his problems for him—that he would be able to have his baby and get rid of his gold-digging wife in one fell swoop!

At the moment he looked like that saying—'found a penny but lost a pound'.

Although quite what the 'penny' and the 'pound' were in all of this Hebe had no idea…!

CHAPTER ELEVEN

'CHEER up, Nick,' Hebe told him lightly, as they drove away from the doctor's consulting rooms two hours later. 'It might never happen!'

It already had, as far as he was concerned.

Neil Adams's prognosis had been excellent, assuring them that Hebe probably would not have the same problem during childbirth as her mother had, and that even if she did, now that he was aware of it, he was sure they could deal with it when the time came. He had told them to just go away until next month, when he would examine Hebe again, and enjoy the pregnancy.

Something Nick hadn't let Hebe do too much of so far!

Admittedly, they had only known about it for a few days, but Nick was all too aware that he had made those days pretty miserable for Hebe.

Even if she *did* seem bright and bubbly now!

He was still slightly in shock over discovering that the portrait *had* been of another woman, after all. Claudia—Hebe's mother.

How stunned Hebe must have been when he'd produced that portrait, knowing it wasn't her even as Nick accused her of all manner of indiscretions.

God, it made him cringe to remember the awful things he had said to her!

Accusations he certainly owed her an apology for.

But he owed her more than that, he acknowledged heavily. He owed Hebe the offer of her freedom, along with his support, emotionally and financially, during her pregnancy and after...

She had been so adamant on Thursday that she wasn't pregnant, so convinced that she couldn't be, and she must have been totally shellshocked when the tests had shown that she was.

And what had *he* done? Armed with the knowledge—so he'd thought—that Hebe had once been engaged to Jacob Gardner and then had had an unsuccessful affair with Andrew Southern, he had accused her of getting pregnant on purpose in order to trap herself a millionaire husband, that was what he had done!

When what he should have been doing was assuring her that everything would work out fine, that he would look after her during her pregnancy, telling her that she would have no worries after the baby was born either, because he would care for both of them.

He should have made all those offers without conditions, without even thinking she might want to marry him, let alone forcing her into doing so!

He glanced at her briefly now, appreciative of just how beautiful she was. It was odd, but she appeared even more so since the doctor had confirmed her pregnancy. She seemed to have taken on that inner glow, her eyes deeply golden, her face creamy and flushed.

She was everything and more that he could ever want in a wife, he realised. She had shown herself to be loyal and loving where her parents were concerned, understanding of the youthful mother who had died giving her life, and, most of all, she had put up with his boorish behaviour when inside she must have felt like screaming her innocence at him.

Yes, Hebe was just too good for him, and he had to let her go.

Nick didn't look too happy, Hebe had to acknowledge, wondering what he could possibly be scowling about so darkly.

'I do believe that Claudia was just a rebellious teenager who got into a situation way over her head…' she began tentatively.

'Could we leave this for now, Hebe?' Nick rasped curtly. 'Obviously we need to talk, but I would rather wait until we get back ho—to the apartment,' he corrected harshly.

She grimaced at this noticeable change of word. 'I was only trying to explain to you that I'm well past the rebellious teenager stage. So you needn't fear a repeat of my mother's behaviour.'

Nick shot her a narrow-eyed glance. 'Claudia was just a kid.'

'Exactly.' Hebe nodded. 'I just thought I would mention it, in case you think that sort of behaviour is hereditary too.'

If it were possible, Nick now looked even more unapproachable.

Personally, she was relieved to have the truth out in the open.

Her parents had returned home to Cambridgeshire soon after the four of them had sat down for a snack lunch Hebe had prepared—with Hebe's promise that she would call them later, to let them know how she had got on at the doctor's.

Strangely, Hebe felt closer to her parents than ever now that she knew they were actually her grandparents, and her mother had promised to get out all the old photographs of Claudia the next time Hebe went home. Hebe felt more as if Claudia had been a sister rather than her mother—the age difference between them was really not that great.

And the child she was expecting would help to bridge any lingering awkwardness there might be at the truth at last being told, binding them all together as a family.

Although Hebe wasn't sure, after a sideways glance at Nick's uncompromising face, that he still wanted to be a part of that family...

She wasn't in the least reassured once they got back to the apartment. Instead of sitting down, Nick paced up and down the room like a caged tiger.

'What is it, Nick?' she finally prompted with a sigh. 'Do you want to call the wedding off? Is that it?'

He stopped his pacing to look at her. 'Is that what you want?'

Her heart sank. She had only asked the question half-heartedly, sure that Nick would still want to marry her, if only to gain complete access to his child.

Then she remembered Sally's telephone call the previous evening and her spirits sank.

She stiffened defensively. 'I asked you first.'

He gave a humourless smile. 'Let's not play that particular game, shall we?' He looked down at her grimly. 'What do you want, Hebe?'

She wanted him!

But she wanted *all* of him, heart and soul, not just the small part of himself he was willing to give her.

And she knew he didn't have it to give. She knew that part of him still belonged to Sally...

He was more remote than he had ever seemed before—the expression on his rakishly handsome face arrogantly distant, not even the denims and casual blue polo-neck he had changed into before they went out making him seem accessible.

Something had changed since last night, and she didn't believe it was only what they now knew about Claudia. Nick's mood had been dark before they had discovered that, which only left Sally's telephone call.

Why didn't she answer him, damn it? Nick brooded impatiently. Why didn't she tell him exactly what she thought of him, and the way he had treated her, and then just walk out of here? It was what he deserved, after all.

He forced his expression to relax. 'I'm willing to go along with whatever it is you want, Hebe,' he assured her quietly.

She continued to look at him for several long seconds, drawing in a ragged breath before answering him. 'Do you believe me when I tell you that I didn't intentionally get pregnant, that it was as much of a surprise to me as it was to you?'

'I believe you.' He nodded. 'I'm sorry that I ever accused you of behaving any differently. I apologise. Most sincerely. There's simply no excuse for the things I've said, the things I've done.' He ran a hand over his eyes. 'You have every reason to hate me.'

'I don't hate you, Nick,' she mused ruefully. 'You're the father of my baby, after all.'

Yes, he was. He was most certainly that. And even if he couldn't hold on to Hebe, he could still continue to see her through their child.

It wouldn't be enough. It would never be enough. But if it was all she was willing to give him he knew he would have to accept that.

It was too late, far too late, for him to try to woo this woman, he had hurt her and wounded her too much for that ever to be possible.

'I *am* sorry, Hebe,' he breathed shakily.

She was very pale now. 'Don't be,' she assured him gently. 'I—I'll go now, then?' she prompted softly.

Nick wanted to get down on his knees, to beg her not to go, and convince her that it would all be so different if she would only stay with him. But that wouldn't be fair of him. He had already messed up her life enough by giving her a child she had neither expected nor wanted, without adding to her misery.

'Will you ever be able to forgive me?' He couldn't stop himself from groaning.

'We can't choose where we love, Nick,' she said flatly. 'It's either there or it isn't.'

And Nick could see that it most certainly wasn't there for Hebe where he was concerned!

Maybe this was his punishment for treating her the way he had. To love a woman who would never, ever love him in return.

Hebe just wanted to get this conversation over with. She couldn't stand it any more. She was sure now that Nick was going back to New York to be with Sally. He would make himself financially responsible for their child, but that was it.

Maybe it was better that it had happened now, before the two of them had made the mistake of getting married— but she just didn't know how she was going to bear it.

Nick would pop in and out of her life and the baby's, a virtual stranger to both of them, his life and his love elsewhere.

Was this how it had been for Claudia? In love with Andrew Southern but rejected by him, and discarded by Jacob Gardner, too, when he'd discovered her relationship with the other man?

But Claudia had only been eighteen years of age, whereas *she* was twenty-six and, as she had told Nick on more than one occasion, more than capable of taking care of herself.

She certainly wasn't going to ask for the love of a man who couldn't be with her because he still loved his first wife!

She stood up abruptly. 'I really think I should go now, Nick. I'll just go and pack my things. Thank goodness Gina hasn't had time yet to find another flatmate,' she added as an attempt at a joke. But her smile and the rest of her face felt as if they were rigidly set.

'I'll drive you back to your apartment—'

'That really isn't necessary—'

'Necessary or not, I intend doing it,' Nick insisted determinedly. 'It's the least I can do,' he added.

'Okay, then. Thank you,' she accepted softly.

They both looked as if they had been through a war—and lost, Hebe decided as she went through to the spare bedroom to collect her things. She hadn't really had time to unpack yet. Five minutes to throw her things back in the case, and she would be out of here.

Out of Nick's life for good.

She only hoped she'd manage to hold back the tears until she was safely back at the flat. It would be just too humiliating if she were to start crying in front of him.

She didn't belong here anyway, she decided with a last look around the beautiful bedroom with its four-poster bed. Neither she nor the baby belonged here.

'Let me take that for you,' Nick said, and he took the suitcase out of Hebe's hand when she came back from the bedroom. 'I—I have the portrait ready for you to take, too,' he added calmly, indicating it wrapped on the sofa and ready to go.

He hadn't been sure what to do about Claudia's portrait. He had thought of offering it to the Johnsons before they left, but it hadn't seemed quite appropriate somehow. But for Hebe, for the moment, it was the only picture she had of her mother, and it surely belonged with her.

He didn't need the portrait to be reminded of Hebe, anyway. He knew he would have the image of her inside his head every day for the rest of his life.

Hebe looked startled by the offer. 'Oh, I couldn't,' she refused stiltedly. 'I—it's an original Andrew Southern, worth a lot of money. Show it in your gallery or something—' she added awkwardly.

'It belongs to you, Hebe,' Nick cut in firmly. 'Not in a public gallery.'

She had taken just about all she could take from him today. She was holding on to her emotions by a very thin thread, and now she knew that he didn't want even Claudia's portrait in his apartment as a reminder of the mistake he had almost made.

'Frightened you might get all the men panting over a portrait of the grandmother of your son or daughter, Nick?' she taunted.

He deserved that, Nick decided heavily. And more.

'I just want you to have it, Hebe,' he answered abruptly. 'It belongs to you and your family.'

But as Nick had said, it was hardly the sort of portrait she could hang over the fireplace in the family sitting room!

'Fine,' she accepted tersely. 'I suppose I can always sell it one day, and put the money into trust for our son or daughter.'

Nick winced slightly. 'I will provide for our child, Hebe. As I will provide for you.'

Hebe shook her head. 'Only until I can go back to work again, and earn my own living. No need to pay for the mistake twice,' she added derisively.

'Our baby is not a mistake!' he snapped impatiently, his handsome face livid with anger.

Hebe eyed him ruefully. 'I was talking about me, Nick, not the baby.'

His dark brows were low over his narrowed blue eyes. 'You weren't a mistake either, Hebe,' he muttered gruffly.

Hebe knew she was something he was going to have to explain to Sally when he returned to New York and the two of them had that 'talk'. She only hoped the other woman would understand, would accept that he hadn't compounded his mistake by actually marrying Hebe.

Which reminded her… 'I'll leave it up to you to see that the wedding arrangements are cancelled.' After all, except for the day and time, she didn't really know what those arrangements were, anyway.

'I'll see to that—yes.' He nodded tersely. 'Now, can we get the hell out of here?' he rasped impatiently. 'I've never liked goodbyes, and this one is— Let's just go, huh?' He ran a hand through the long thickness of his hair.

'You'll be wanting this back, too.' Hebe started to take the yellow sapphire and diamond ring off her finger.

'Will you please stop adding insult to injury?' Nick snapped forcefully, glaring down at her. 'The ring is yours. The portrait is yours. And anything else I can get you to accept from me will be yours, too.'

But not his heart.

Not his love.

Which was all she really wanted...

But pride could only take her so far, and she knew that in the months ahead she was going to need Nick's financial help, at least. She wished she were in a position to turn away that offer of help, but she wasn't—not without becoming a burden to her parents. It was no good even pretending she was.

'Fine,' she accepted tersely. 'I'm ready to go if you are.' She nodded.

Nick wasn't sure he would ever be ready to help Hebe leave his life in this way. But he also knew he didn't have a choice. Because he had done this to himself.

If only he hadn't seen that portrait and assumed it was Hebe. If only he had listened to her when she'd told him it wasn't her. If only he hadn't acted on the assumption that she had already tried to entrap two wealthy men and failed. He'd believed that he was just the third in line, with the added inducement of pregnancy before the marriage this time. If he hadn't, maybe he would have been able to ask Hebe to give him a second chance.

But he *had* done all of those things.

And Hebe walking out of his life was exactly what he deserved!

Hebe could quite easily have broken down and cried on the journey to her flat, staring out through the side window of the car as she blinked back those ready tears, determined she had to hold on until after Nick had left her—because she couldn't let him see how much this parting from him was hurting her.

She didn't even know when she was going to see him again.

Or if.

Nick might just decide to handle all the financial details through his lawyers, and eventual access to the baby would be handled in the same way.

Even being forced into marrying Nick would be better than never knowing when or if she would ever see him again!

She turned to him after unlocking the door to her flat. 'Can I continue to work at the gallery until—until—'

'Work at the gallery as long as you want to—or not. Whatever you decide to do,' he came back curtly. 'I'll instruct Jane as such when I get back.'

'I just—'

'Hebe, can we go inside? This portrait weighs a ton!' He grimaced, resting the painting against his knee. 'I've probably given myself a hernia carrying it up the stairs as it is!'

She smiled. 'You—'

'Excuse me,' a voice behind them interrupted. 'I'm looking for Flat—' The voice broke of abruptly.

Hebe had turned at the first query, her gaze becoming quizzical as the man stopped speaking, his face slowly draining of colour as he just stood and stared at her.

'Claudia...?' the man gasped disbelievingly.

There was only one man Hebe could think of who might mistake her for her mother.

But it couldn't be—!

CHAPTER TWELVE

'ANDREW SOUTHERN?' Nick enquired, as neither Hebe nor the man staring at her with a dazed look seemed able to speak.

'Yes,' the artist confirmed in a strangulated voice, not taking his gaze from Hebe for a moment.

Nick knew how the other man felt—he didn't want to stop looking at Hebe either!

But he knew the other man's fascination with Hebe was for quite another reason than his own...

He recognised Andrew Southern from photographs he had seen, although he was older now, of course, the dark hair heavily peppered with grey, his handsome face weathered and lined, his eyes a deep, piercing grey.

Hebe's father. Or not.

It didn't really matter at that moment; the other man had cared enough, after receiving Hebe's letter, to come to London in person rather than just writing back or telephoning.

Hebe couldn't be unaware of the relevance of that either.

Hebe swallowed hard, unable to move or stop looking at the man who might be her real father. The two of them simply stared at each other.

Andrew Southern was the first to recover, shaking his

head ruefully. 'Of course you aren't Claudia,' he murmured gruffly. 'You're far too young to be her. But the likeness... the likeness—' He stopped as his voice broke emotionally.

'Uncanny, isn't it?' Nick said bitterly.

Hebe knew it was this likeness that had resulted in him making such a mistake where she was concerned—and Nick wasn't a man who liked to make mistakes.

'My name is Hebe,' she told the older man huskily. 'You received my letter?'

'Yes,' he breathed, and Hebe looked at him again. He was a man aged in his early fifties, tall and handsome, with grey eyes that seemed to see into the soul.

An artist's eyes, Hebe decided. Eyes that saw beyond the outer shell of a person into the very heart of them. As he had once seen beyond Claudia's youthful recklessness...?

'Would you like to come inside?' she invited shyly as she pushed the flat door open, aware of Nick standing back until the older man had entered, and then following behind carrying the portrait.

The portrait...!

Nick anticipated Hebe's request, placing the portrait on the table before removing the covering, then turning to look at the older man as he propped the portrait against the wall.

Andrew Southern went even paler, seemingly possessed by the same stupor as first Hebe and then her parents had been on seeing the portrait.

The difference was that this man had actually painted the picture, already knew every loving brushstroke, every soft nuance and shading of Claudia's beautiful face and body.

'I never thought I would see this portrait again,' Andrew

Southern murmured as he gazed at it in wonder. 'How did you get it?' he breathed raggedly.

Nick was the one to answer him. 'I bought it from Jacob Gardner's great-nephew after he died.'

'Claudia!' Andrew's voice broke emotionally. 'I tried to buy it back from Jacob Gardner myself after—after Claudia left. But he refused to sell it to me.'

'He never married,' Nick told him quietly.

'No.' Andrew sighed. 'How could any man after Claudia? My darling Claudia…!' He buried his face in his hands and began to sob.

This man, Nick knew with startling clarity, had loved Claudia with the same depth, the same deep need, with which *he* now loved Hebe.

But for some as yet unexplained reason Andrew had lost his Claudia.

Was Nick really going to allow the same thing to happen to him where Hebe was concerned?

'I'm so sorry,' Hebe murmured, and she moved forward to put a hand on Andrew Southern's shaking shoulders.

The artist looked up with a tear-ravaged face. '*You're* sorry?' he choked self-derisively. 'I let this wonderful creature slip through my fingers like molten gold, and you're sorry?' He gave a self-disgusted shake of his head. 'I should have acted sooner than I did. Should never—' He broke off. 'I've spent the last twenty-six years aching for just another glimpse of her, just to see her smile in that mischievous way of hers, to be able to hold her one more time!'

No! Nick cried inwardly. He was not going to live his own life in that way—give Hebe up without even telling her how he felt about her. And if he tried hard enough he just might—might!—be able to convince her into caring for him with even a little of the deep love he felt for her.

'Claudia is the reason you stopped appearing in public?' Hebe prompted softly. 'The reason you stopped painting portraits, too?' she realized, with sudden insight.

'Losing Claudia is the reason I gave up those things, yes,' Andrew Southern confirmed gruffly. 'I changed my life completely after what I had done!'

Hebe looked at him quizzically. 'What did you do?'

He shook his head. 'Claudia was engaged to marry Jacob Gardner when he commissioned me to paint her portrait, and I was married—if not happily—but it made no difference. We—we took one look at each other and neither Jacob nor my wife seemed to matter any more.'

At last Hebe had a possible explanation as to why Claudia, after breaking off her engagement to Jacob Gardner, had left alone rather than with Andrew Southern. Because he'd already had a wife…

'But why, if you loved each other, did you let her go off alone like that to have her baby?' She frowned. 'Or didn't you love her enough to leave your wife, is that it?'

All of this was starting to have a familiar ring to it as far as Hebe was concerned. History repeating itself. Well, not quite, she corrected herself. Nick didn't love her, but he was leaving her to have her baby alone and going back to his ex-wife.

'Of course I loved her enough to leave my wife!' His eyes glittered emotionally. 'But we argued. Claudia—she didn't believe me when I said I would end my marriage to be with her. But I did end it. And I went to see her the same day to tell her I had, that I only wanted to be with her, wanted her to come and live with me. She didn't tell me she was pregnant!' Andrew groaned fiercely. 'She had been there the day before, but when I went back the next day to tell her I couldn't live without her, that I loved her, she—she had gone. I never saw her again.' He closed his eyes as if to shut out the pain.

Except Nick knew that the older man couldn't do that, and he couldn't either. The image of Andrew's Claudia, and Hebe for him, couldn't be shut out. It was etched into the brain for all time.

Claudia and Hebe were women the men in their lives loved for a lifetime.

Jacob Gardner had continued to love Claudia even after she had betrayed and then left him. The portrait in his bedroom after all those years was evidence of that. And Andrew Southern's pain at losing his Claudia was unmistakable. Nick knew without doubt that he loved Hebe in that same all-consuming way.

'I—' Hebe paused, moistening suddenly dry lips. 'You realise I'm Claudia's baby?' she asked Andrew Southern warily.

He gave a choked laugh as he looked at her. 'You couldn't be anyone else!' He reached up a shaking hand to touch her cheek lightly. 'You are so like her,' he breathed softly. 'So very, very like her.'

Hebe shot Nick a rueful glance. 'Yes.'

A glance he returned with a glittering determination she didn't understand. But then, she never had understood Nick, so why should that change now, when he was shortly going to go out of her life for good?

She turned back to Andrew Southern. 'The question is—' she grimaced '—am I your daughter or Jacob Gardner's?'

'Mine, of course!' the artist claimed frowningly. 'Claudia—your mother—didn't have that sort of relationship with Jacob Gardner. In fact she had never had that sort of relationship with anyone before me,' he admitted gruffly.

Hebe blinked. 'But—'

'There was no one else before me, Hebe,' he told her firmly. 'Claudia liked to give the impression that she was wild and untamed, that she was worldly-wise, even. But in reality she was a sweet, enchanting young woman who had never been with a man before me. I felt a complete heel when I realised that the first time we made love.' He gave a shaky sigh. 'I wasn't happily married, but that was no excuse for seducing an innocent!'

Hebe didn't really care about that. She just felt happier knowing that her parents' love and care for Claudia hadn't been misplaced at all, and that she really had just been the rebellious teenager Hebe had told Nick she'd been.

Andrew Southern's gaze was pained. 'I tried to find her. I really tried, Hebe.' He looked at her earnestly. 'But she had just disappeared.'

Hebe gave a tearful smile. 'I don't think she intended you to find her—or anyone else, in fact.' She drew in a deep breath. 'I didn't know when I wrote to you on Friday, but—but Claudia's parents only learnt of her whereabouts when the hospital called them as next of kin. She died giving birth to me,' she explained as gently as she could. 'They brought me up, and have been the only parents I've never known.'

Andrew gave another choked sob. 'All these years… I never knew what had happened to her, Hebe. Why she left so suddenly,' he explained as she looked puzzled. 'Until I received your letter this morning and saw that photograph of you I never knew that she was expecting my child. And it never—it never even occurred to me that she might have been dead all these years.' He gave a disbelieving shake of his head, as if he still couldn't take it all in.

Nick looked at the other man admiringly, not sure he would be staying even this much together if he had just learnt that Hebe was dead.

'Or that you had a daughter?' Hebe put in softly.

Andrew Southern's face lit up as he looked at her, but the sorrow remained etched beside his eyes and mouth. 'Or that I have the gift of a daughter. A very beautiful daughter,' he added gruffly.

'Who, in seven months' time, is going to make you a grandfather,' Nick added gently, and he stepped forward to place his arm possessively about Hebe's shoulders.

She gave him a surprised look. What was Nick doing? Andrew Southern—her father—didn't need to know about the baby she was expecting. It served no purpose at this moment, and would surely make it more difficult for Nick to just walk away, as he intended doing.

Andrew Southern looked at the younger man with sharply assessing eyes. 'And am I going to have to get my shotgun oiled and ready…?' he finally murmured derisively.

'No,' Nick answered firmly. 'Hebe and I are getting married. If she'll have me…?' He turned to look down at her uncertainly.

She swallowed hard, shaking her head, not understanding this at all.

'Looks like you have some persuading to do there, Nick.' Andrew had misinterpreted that dazed shake of her head as a refusal. 'Feel free to take her off somewhere private. I'm quite happy sitting here looking at Claudia's portrait for an hour or six—or a lifetime,' he added, and he sat down in the armchair beside the painting, already seeming to have forgotten their existence as his eyes misted tearfully and the tears began to fall for the woman he had loved and would never see again.

Hebe took Nick into the room that had used to be her bedroom, bare now of everything that marked it as being hers, not understanding what was going on at all.

'Do you think he's going to be all right?' She frowned with concern.

'I think that he's probably had twenty-six years to come to terms with losing Claudia, so her death makes it no more final,' Nick answered carefully. 'With your agreement, I would like to give him the portrait of Claudia? It belongs with him, don't you think?'

'Yes,' she answered, slightly breathlessly, appreciating his understanding. 'Oh, yes! But I—I thought we had agreed to cancel the wedding.' She looked up at him, puzzled. 'I told you, I'm not going to be difficult—'

'I am,' he cut in grimly, his dark blue gaze fixed firmly on hers. 'Hebe, I don't intend ending up like Andrew—in love with a woman for the rest of my life but not *with* her.'

'I realise that,' she acknowledged softly. 'That's why I agreed to end the engagement, and forget our marriage. I know you and Sally want to be reconciled—'

'Sally?' Nick cut in sharply. 'What the hell does *Sally* have to do with any of this?'

Hebe looked confused. 'I didn't mean to, but I overheard you talking to her on the telephone yesterday evening.' She swallowed hard. 'I know she's the reason you no longer want a marriage of convenience with me—that the two of you want to be together and that you're going to talk things over when you go back to New York.'

Nick looked at her incredulously. *That* was why, after the two of them had made love so beautifully, so thoroughly, Hebe had gone to the spare room to sleep last night! The reason she had been so ready to call off the engagement and cancel the wedding. Because she thought he was still in love with Sally!

'Hebe.' He breathed deeply. 'Sally remarried a year ago, very happily. Last night she called to tell me—she was so happy she had to share it with me—that she had just given birth to a little girl.' He watched Hebe closely for her reaction. 'I probably should have told you about it, but you had gone from my bedroom when I got back, and in the morning— Well, you know what it was like between us this morning.'

Hebe stared at him incredulously. 'Sally's had a *baby*…?'

'Yes.' He nodded, hope starting to blossom and grow.

'Hebe, I know you might find this hard to believe after the way I've behaved—' he shook his head self-disgustedly '—but the only woman I want to be with, the only woman I love, will *ever* love, is you!'

Hebe's incredulity turned to wonder. 'You do…?'

'I do,' he assured her grimly. 'I think I fell in love with you six weeks ago. These last two years, when I've been—involved with a woman, I've just forgotten about her once I've walked away,' he admitted ruefully. 'But you—you were different. I thought about nothing but you for five weeks—six if you count the week after I bought the portrait. I knew even then that I would have to see you again once I returned to London, that somehow you had got under my skin.'

Hebe moistened her dry lips, hardly able to believe Nick was saying these things to her. 'But the portrait changed all that…?'

He nodded, sighing. 'Because I'm an idiot. Because I didn't believe you when you told me you weren't the woman in the portrait. It looked like you!' he groaned. 'The you I had seen the night we spent together. The you who had been like a living flame in my arms. The you who had been haunting my days and invading my nights.' He shook his head. 'Seeing that portrait, imagining the man who had painted it looking at you and seeing exactly what I had seen, touching you in the way I had touched you— I was so angry I think I was blind with rage the next time we met,' he admitted.

Nick *was* saying these things to her!

'And now?' she prompted breathlessly. 'Now that you know the truth? You released me from our engagement and agreed to cancel the wedding,' she reminded him huskily.

He gave a humourless smile. 'I was trying to do the honourable thing. I realised that I had bullied you into both those things because of my mistaken belief that you were trying to trap me into marriage by getting pregnant on purpose. And I *was* mistaken, Hebe. I know now that you were just as surprised by your pregnancy as I was. Worse, you were probably terrified. And I've behaved like a complete bastard to you,' he murmured self-disgustedly.

'But now?' she prompted again.

'Now, after listening to Andrew, hearing him describe how much he loved Claudia and the hell his life has been for him since he lost her, I've decided—unless I want to go quietly insane—that I have to forget being honourable,' he said determinedly. 'I don't want to be another Jacob or Andrew, my life barren and loveless because I've let the woman I love walk away from me without even trying to show her how much I love her and want to be with her. If it takes me months, or even years, I'm going to woo you, Hebe Johnson.' He reached out to grasp her arms. 'I'm going to woo you and win you. I love you too much, need you too much, to ever be able to let you just walk away from me. Will you allow me to do that, Hebe?' he pressed fiercely. 'Will you give me a chance to court you, care for you, love you?'

Hebe almost laughed at the ridiculousness of that question—she already loved him so much that parting from him today had been like a nightmare she couldn't awaken from!

'No, I don't think so, Nick,' she told him emotionally. 'No, I don't mean it like that!' she hastened to assure him as he went deathly pale. 'You see, I already love you.' She smiled. 'I've loved you for months—before you even spoke to me the first time,' she admitted joyously. 'And if it's all right with you, I would like to go ahead with our wedding!'

'Hebe…?' He looked at her in disbelief..

'I love you, Nick!' It felt so good to be able to say those words at last—to let her love for this man shine in her eyes and light up her face. 'I love you, and I want to spend the rest of my life with you!'

Nick stared down at her as he drew in a shaky breath. 'For eternity.' He spoke forcefully. 'I'm not willing to settle for anything less!'

'Eternity,' she echoed with a happy laugh. 'I'm not willing to settle for anything less either!'

'I swear to you that we're going to be happy together, Hebe,' Nick assured her firmly. 'So very, very happy.'

She believed him.

And when their son and daughter, Andrew Henry and Claudia Luka, were born seven months later, mother and babies all healthy, Hebe knew she had been right to trust and believe in Nick—that their love for each other just grew stronger each and every day they were together.

As it would for eternity.

MILLS & BOON®

Live the emotion

Modern
romance™

THE SPANIARD'S MARRIAGE DEMAND
by Maggie Cox

Leandro Reyes could have any girl he wanted. Only in the cold light of morning did Isabella realise she was just another notch on his bed-post. But their passion had a consequence Leandro couldn't ignore. His solution: to demand Isabella marry him!

THE PRINCE'S CONVENIENT BRIDE
by Robyn Donald

Prince Marco Considine knows he's met his match when he sees model Jacoba Sinclair. But Jacoba has a secret: she's Illyrian, like Prince Marco, a fact that could endanger her life. Marco seizes the opportunity to protect her...by announcing their engagement!

ONE-NIGHT BABY *by Susan Stephens*

Five years ago, virginal Kate Mulhoon met top Hollywood producer Santino Rossi – but he knew nothing of her innocence, or of the baby they made that one night together... Now Santino is determined to find out what Kate's hiding, and once he does he *will* make her his...

THE RICH MAN'S RELUCTANT MISTRESS
by Margaret Mayo

Interior decorator Lucinda Oliver's latest client is gorgeous playboy Zane Alexander. Lucinda's determined not to be one of his conquests... But when their work takes them to the Caribbean, she's seduced by the exotic surroundings – and Zane's sizzling desire...

On sale 2nd March 2007

Available at WHSmith, Tesco, ASDA, and all good bookshops

www.millsandboon.co.uk

0207/01b

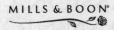

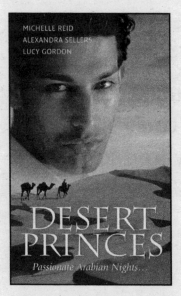

FREE

4 BOOKS AND A SURPRISE GIFT!

We would like to take this opportunity to thank you for reading this Mills & Boon® book by offering you the chance to take FOUR more specially selected titles from the Modern Romance™ series absolutely FREE! We're also making this offer to introduce you to the benefits of the Mills & Boon® Reader Service™—

    ★ **FREE home delivery**
    ★ **FREE gifts and competitions**
    ★ **FREE monthly Newsletter**
    ★ **Books available before they're in the shops**
    ★ **Exclusive Reader Service offers**

Accepting these FREE books and gift places you under no obligation to buy; you may cancel at any time, even after receiving your free shipment. Simply complete your details below and return the entire page to the address below. You don't even need a stamp!

YES! Please send me 4 free Modern Romance books and a surprise gift. I understand that unless you hear from me, I will receive 6 superb new titles every month for just £2.80 each, postage and packing free. I am under no obligation to purchase any books and may cancel my subscription at any time. The free books and gift will be mine to keep in any case.

P7ZEE

Ms/Mrs/Miss/Mr..................................Initials ....
                                                             BLOCK CAPITALS PLEASE

Surname ....

Address ....

....

....Postcode ....

Send this whole page to:
The Reader Service, FREEPOST CN81, Croydon, CR9 3WZ